Romance 101

"There's another test coming up soon," Monsieur LeBlanc told Samantha Daley. "We'd better see that you receive tutoring. When do you have free time?"

"Any night," Samantha said quickly.

"I'll work something out," Marc LeBlanc said, jotting a note to himself.

"Thank you so much," Samantha said as they headed for the door together.

"No problem." Marc smiled at her then. It wasn't just his friendly-teacher smile, either, Samantha told herself. No, this time his eyes were definitely sparkling. Samantha was sure there was a deeper meaning in his expression. He really cared about her, she knew.

"Don't worry, Samantha," Marc said. "We'll get through this."

We certainly will, Samantha thought happily. Together.

Books in the River Heights ™ Series

Available from ARCHWAY Paperbacks

River HEIGHTS #6

LESSONS IN LOVE

CAROLYN KEENE

AN ARCHWAY PAPERBACK
Published by POCKET BOOKS
New York   London   Toronto   Sydney   Tokyo   Singapore

AN ARCHWAY PAPERBACK *Original*

An Archway Paperback published by
POCKET BOOKS, a division of Simon & Schuster Inc.
1230 Avenue of the Americas, New York, NY 10020

Copyright © 1990 by Simon & Schuster Inc.
Cover art copyright © 1990 Carla Sormanti
Produced by Mega-Books of New York, Inc.

ISBN: 0-671-67764-0

First Archway Paperback printing July 1990

10 9 8 7 6 5 4 3 2 1

AN ARCHWAY PAPERBACK and colophon are registered trademarks of Simon & Schuster Inc.

RIVER HEIGHTS is a trademark of Simon & Schuster Inc.

Printed in the U.S.A.

IL 6 +

LESSONS
IN LOVE

 **1**

Applause, accompanied by whistles and hoots, erupted from the auditorium.

Nikki Masters could hardly believe it. She'd just given the performance of her life as Emily, the female lead, in the River Heights High production of *Our Town.*

Nikki and the rest of the cast scrambled offstage to the wings to get in line for their curtain calls.

She hurried to her spot next to Tim Cooper, her very recent ex-boyfriend. He had played the lead of George Gibbs.

The cast walked onto the stage. Swiping at the beads of perspiration dotting her forehead, Nikki wished she could magically disappear. Standing that close to Tim was practically killing her.

"Nikki, please," Tim whispered, taking her hand for a bow. "You've got to listen to me."

"No!" Nikki whispered back, managing to smile at the audience at the same time.

Applause continued to roll through the auditorium.

"We have to talk!" Tim insisted.

Nikki gently shook her head, her blond hair sweeping the collar of her costume. "Not now!" she told him. "I'm sorry."

The cast ran offstage again, and Nikki pulled her hand away from Tim's.

"Nikki," Tim pleaded. "It wasn't what it looked like!"

Lies, lies, lies. "I really don't want to hear about it." Pain seared through Nikki as she remembered the scene she'd encountered outside the night before at the cast party. Tim and Lara Bennett had been alone, moonlight flooding over them as they embraced. Nikki had surprised the two of them on her way to her car. She had driven away, fighting back tears.

"I'm telling you, Nikki, it wasn't what you think," Tim said, holding her shoulders.

Part of Nikki wanted to believe him. Tim's gray eyes were staring into hers, pleading with her. Tim Cooper had been practically everything in the world to her until the night before.

"Okay, Tim," the stage manager said, breaking in. "You and Nikki. Now."

Tim clasped Nikki's hand in his once again. His fingers were strong and warm. Nikki plastered a smile on her face as the two of them ran out on the stage again. They took sweeping bows before the packed house.

By then the crowd was on its feet. As Tim and Nikki appeared, the applause grew deafening. Someone laid roses at Nikki's feet, and cameras flashed, blinding her.

How long had she waited for just this moment—to share the spotlight onstage with Tim? Now her dreams were shattered. From the corner of her eye she spied Lara Bennett standing nervously in the wings. Nikki looked away quickly and leaned over to pick up the roses. She smiled brightly at the audience, then dashed offstage. Tim was right behind her.

"Nikki! Wait up!" he called. As Nikki hurried into the wings, Tim pushed past other members of the cast. His footsteps echoed loudly against the floorboards of the stage.

Tim finally caught up with Nikki in the

hall leading to the dressing rooms. He grabbed her elbow. "Let me explain about last night," he said.

"I *know* what happened," Nikki told him.

Tim's grip tightened. "No, Nikki, you don't. I swear."

The picture of Lara wrapped in Tim's arms would be stamped forever in Nikki's mind. "Save your story, Tim, for someone stupid enough to believe it!"

She started to pull away, but Tim still held on to her arm. "Nikki, Lara and I are just friends—"

"Is that the way you act with all your friends?" Nikki asked, raising her chin. Tears began to fill the corners of her eyes.

"I was only explaining to Lara about us," Tim said.

"Us?" Nikki repeated, frowning.

"Yes, Nikki. You and me."

Her throat felt thick. If only she could believe him. Then Nikki remembered how Tim had danced with her at the cast party —as if he couldn't wait for the music to end—and then how he'd made a beeline for Lara.

"Tim!" Brittany Tate's voice called from somewhere above them.

Nikki froze. How could she face Brittany, of all people, now? And how long had that girl been standing on the stairs? Had she overheard their conversation?

Nikki closed her eyes and gritted her teeth.

Tim's grip loosened on Nikki's arm as he swung around to face Brittany.

Dressed in a black sweater and red suede miniskirt, Brittany hurried down the steps. Her dark eyes sparkled as she flipped her shining black hair away from her face. "Hi, Tim, Nikki. I just wanted to ask how you two felt about your final performance." Her pouty lips curved upward as she waved a pen and notepad in their faces. "You know, for a follow-up article in the *Record.*"

Nikki squared her shoulders. The last time Brittany had interviewed her for the school paper, Nikki had been battling stage fright. She'd come off sounding like an idiot in the school paper.

"Didn't you see the play?" Tim asked. To Nikki's satisfaction, he sounded annoyed by the interruption.

"Just the end." Brittany slid a look in Nikki's direction. "I didn't see it last night but I saw the entire show opening night," she said, referring to Nikki's less-than-perfect performance on Friday night.

Nikki's chest and throat tightened, but she forced her voice to sound calm. "I think the last two performances went extremely well," she said, managing a thin smile.

Brittany raised her eyebrows.

Tim nodded. "It's too bad it's all over."

Was there a double meaning in his words? "Yes," Nikki echoed, fighting tears. "It's too bad." Then, before the situation deteriorated even further, she forced a smile. "Listen, Brittany, I've really got to go. If you have any more questions, you can call me at home." With a quick wave, Nikki raised her long white skirt slightly and raced toward the girls' dressing room.

She slammed the door behind her and tore off her costume, ignoring the other girls' excited chatter. She never wanted to think about *Our Town* or Tim Cooper again! Her throat hot with unshed tears, Nikki yanked on her favorite jeans and a pink cowl-necked sweater. She didn't even bother with fixing her hair or removing her makeup. The sooner she got out of there, the better.

Nikki slid her arms into her denim jacket and headed out the back exit. She didn't want to risk running into Tim and Brittany again.

Outside, the air was crisp and cold.

Nikki could see her breath in the air as she ran through the parking lot to her car.

You're running away, she told herself as she climbed into the cold, metallic blue Camaro and jammed her key in the ignition. "So what?" she muttered angrily. The engine fired. Nikki put her foot down hard on the gas pedal and the car roared out of the lot. She'd cried her last tears for Tim Cooper!

Brittany Tate, still standing with Tim in the hallway, struggled against an urge to smile. It seemed as if her plan had worked. Tim and Nikki had broken up. The split had begun with Brittany's last article in the *Record*. Not only had she focused the article solely on Tim and Lara, who'd played Mrs. Gibbs in *Our Town,* she'd hinted rather strongly about an offstage romance between them, too.

Then Brittany had taken on the awesome responsibility of making Lara over —teaching the slightly mousy sophomore how to do her hair and use makeup. The transformation in Lara had been amazing, and Tim had definitely noticed.

Right then, though, Brittany had Tim Cooper all to herself.

"Are you okay?" she asked, laying a

hand on Tim's shoulder. He was still staring down the empty hall where Nikki had disappeared.

"I'm fine," he said, though his jaw remained tight.

Tim really was gorgeous, Brittany told herself. With his fantastic gray eyes, thick brown hair, and lean, muscular build, he was definitely the best-looking guy in the junior class.

She raised a concerned brow in his direction. "More trouble with Nikki?"

Tim sighed, running a hand through his hair. "Big trouble."

"Maybe I can help," Brittany offered, trying to sound as sympathetic as she possibly could.

"Thanks, but I don't think so," Tim answered.

"I'd be glad to talk to Nikki for you," Brittany said.

"She's not in the mood for talking," Tim said with a sigh. "Believe me, I've tried."

"Oh, Tim, *there* you are!" Lara Bennett ran toward him. She stopped right in front of Tim and turned adoring eyes up at him.

Brittany wished more than anything that Lara would evaporate, but she gave the younger girl a cool smile. "I was just asking Tim some questions about the final two performances of the play for the *Record."*

Lara beamed. "Really? Maybe I could help, too."

Great, Brittany thought, uncapping her pen. Just what she needed. "Okay, Lara," Brittany said out loud. "I *do* have a question for you." She smiled sweetly. "How did it feel to play the part of a frumpy older woman?"

"What?" Lara frowned.

"I mean, the director must have thought you were better suited for a—well, more *matronly* role. You know, as Tim's mother. Was it hard to play?"

"Uh, n-no. I m-mean, sure," Lara stammered, her color rising.

Brittany felt a twinge of guilt. She didn't blame Lara for being embarrassed. Lara probably considered Brittany a good friend after all the time Brittany had spent with her.

"Well, it doesn't matter," Brittany said quickly. "You did a great job, Lara."

"Thanks."

Lara looked puzzled and relieved, but Tim hardly seemed to notice. He was still staring down the hall.

Marc LeBlanc, Samantha Daley thought dreamily as she sat at her frilly bedroom vanity. Even his name sounded *so* French and sophisticated. She couldn't wait until the next day. So what if the guy was a graduate student at Westmoor University and probably five years older than she? So what if he was going to be her substitute French teacher while that old bag Madame Duval recuperated from her broken hip?

She and Marc were destined to be together. Why else would she have run into him at the ice-cream parlor on Saturday night? It had to be fate. Samantha glanced in the mirror and adjusted her cinnamon-colored waves. She'd have to tame them to look older, she decided. She wound her hair away from her face. A French braid would be perfect. And with a little extra makeup, and her most sophisticated clothes, she really would look older than she was.

Samantha tilted her head this way and that, studying her profile.

Saturday night Marc *had* seemed a little nervous when he'd found out she was only a junior at River Heights High.

Before she had let that damaging piece of news slip out, he'd definitely been interested. Samantha recognized male interest when she saw it—especially if it was cast in her direction. Marc *had* been flirting with her—until he'd found out she wasn't a college student!

Well, that didn't matter all that much, did it?

The phone rang, and Samantha picked up her bedroom extension. "Hello?"

"Hi!" Kim Bishop greeted her. Kim was Samantha's good friend and one of the most popular girls at school. Kim, Samantha, and Brittany Tate stuck together like glue.

"Oh, hi," Samantha said, flopping back on her bed and reluctantly turning her thoughts away from Marc LeBlanc. "What's up?"

"Well, I wanted to let you know. Jeremy's folks are going out of town on a quickie vacation to the Bahamas," Kim said.

Samantha twirled the telephone cord. Jeremy, super snob of River Heights High, was Kim's steady boyfriend.

"He's decided to have a party while they're gone—just a few close friends, of course," Kim went on. "Kids from the country club and a few from school. He asked me to include you."

Samantha glanced up at the calendar on her bulletin board. "When?"

"Two weeks from Friday." Kim's voice

lowered a little. "This will be a party to remember," she said. "I wouldn't miss it, if I were you."

"Wouldn't dream of it," Samantha said, wondering if she could work that fast. She'd have to have a date, naturally. Her eyes narrowed. What would it take to get Marc LeBlanc to ask her out? And even if he did, would he want to go to a party with a bunch of high school kids? Not likely.

"There'll be plenty of guys there," Kim went on, but Samantha was barely listening. She wasn't interested in any of the immature jerks from River Heights High — not now, anyway.

Kim wouldn't let up. "I'm sure I could ask one of Jeremy's buddies to pick you up."

Samantha couldn't believe her ears. A date with one of Jeremy Pratt's rich-rat friends? No way! She *did* have standards, after all. She couldn't say that to Kim and hurt Kim's feelings, though.

"I'll bring my own date," Samantha said casually, coiling the phone cord around her fingers.

"A new guy?" Kim sounded interested. "You haven't told me anything about him."

"Mmm," Samantha replied noncommittally. She couldn't confide in Kim yet. Not until she'd found a way to get Marc to ask her out.

"Who is it?" Kim persisted.

"Oh, no one you know," Samantha said evasively, staring at the polish on her nails. She was kind of enjoying this little game with Kim.

"Well, by all means, bring the guy," Kim told her. "Just as long as he's not some geek."

"A *geek?*" Samantha was insulted. "Don't you know me better than that?"

"Well, you know what I mean," Kim said quickly. "Jeremy is incredibly particular about who shows up at his house."

Samantha bristled. "Tell him not to worry, okay?"

"So is this new mystery man going to take you to the dance?" Kim asked. "It's this Friday, remember."

Samantha thought quickly. Marc Le-Blanc wouldn't be caught dead at a high school dance. "Well, I don't know," she answered mysteriously. "We may be doing something else that night. Listen, I've got to go, Kim."

Kim sounded a bit miffed. "Okay, fine," she said. "I'll see you in school then, I guess."

"I guess so," Samantha said. "See you tomorrow. 'Bye." She made a very con-

scious effort not to slam down the phone.
Kim could be extremely annoying.

Samantha headed straight for her closet
and began digging through every piece of
clothing. She had to look extra sophisticated at school that week.

She pulled out a black T-shirt dress and
smiled to herself. Kim and Brittany would
both die of shock and envy when she
showed up at Jeremy's party with the most
incredible male in River Heights!

As for Marc LeBlanc . . . Samantha
glanced back at the mirror and showed her
dimples prettily. By the time she was
through with him, Monsieur Gorgeous
wouldn't know what had hit him!

2

"Who is *that*?" Brittany whispered. Her gaze followed the figure of a tall, lean young man as he strode quickly across the parking lot toward the school.

"Oh, him?" Samantha replied casually. Her brown eyes avoided Brittany's as she tugged open the door of River Heights High and walked quickly inside. "He's a graduate student at Westmoor, I think. He's substituting for old Madame Duval until she's back on her feet," she threw over her shoulder.

"He's a teacher?" Brittany shrugged. "*Our* teacher? Too bad."

Brittany practically had to run through the crowded halls of the north wing of

River Heights to keep up with Samantha. "So what else do you know about this guy?"

"Nothing," Samantha replied quickly. "Look, Brittany, I've really got to hurry. I can't afford any more late slips." With that, she took off through the crowded hallway, leaving Brittany standing with her mouth half-open.

"Did I miss something?" Kim Bishop asked, gazing after Samantha.

"I'm not sure," Brittany replied slowly. Samantha had been very preoccupied on the drive to school that morning, and her white leather miniskirt and short jacket were a little much for school. Brittany's eyes narrowed as she thought.

Kim waved to someone in the distance. "You know, Samantha sounded a little weird on the phone last night," she said. "I offered to set her up with one of Jeremy's friends for his party, but she said she was bringing her own date."

Brittany raised her eyebrows. "Really?"

"I wonder who he is," Kim mused as the crush of students around them slowly thinned out.

"So do I," Brittany said. A suspicion was beginning to form in her mind. Samantha had practically bolted at the mention of the new French teacher. Could it be possible? Brittany decided not to say anything to Kim until she was sure. For once, French class might prove interesting.

Samantha dived into the rest room. A few sophomore girls were hanging around the mirror, gossiping, but Samantha pushed her way to the front and studied her reflection. Did her hair look okay? Was her outfit too much? Would Marc LeBlanc realize that she was more mature than most of the girls at River Heights High?

Samantha touched up her mascara, which had clumped a little, and forced a cool smile to her lips. The other girls left, but Samantha barely noticed.

She was ready to prove to Marc that she could hold her own against any college girl. She tucked a stray lock of hair into her neatly twisted French braid. Samantha knew she was pretty, and she used her good looks to her advantage. Hadn't she been taking lessons from Brittany for a while? It would be only a matter of time before Monsieur LeBlanc was snagged.

The door to the rest room burst open, and a small group of girls entered. Samantha immediately recognized Nikki Masters and Nikki's best friends, Robin Fisher and Lacey Dupree.

Nikki, blond and blue eyed, oozed charm and style. Because of her family's wealth and social position—Samantha reminded herself—the girl could well afford to be nice. Robin, however, with her short dark hair and outrageous fashion sense, was always shooting off her mouth. And fair, redheaded Lacey Dupree, a total spacehead in Samantha's opinion, was almost as bad. Brittany had nicknamed them the Moose and the Mouse.

Nikki grinned at Samantha's reflection and gave a little wave. Samantha offered her new, sophisticated half-smile in return. Then, without a word, she picked up her bag and headed out the door. How could she ever wait until French class? She knew she'd die before then!

"What was *her* problem?" Robin asked as the door swung closed behind Samantha.

"Who cares?" Lacey said with a shrug. "She's a snob."

Nikki, too, had felt the snub, but she couldn't worry about Samantha Daley right then. Not when her world was falling apart.

"Okay, let's hear it," Robin said, tossing her dark hair away from her face. She crossed her arms over her chest and leaned against a sink. "Why is Tim being so awful?"

Nikki sighed. "He was with Lara Bennett at the cast party."

"A lot of people were there, right?" Robin pointed out.

"I know, but Tim and Lara were outside together. He actually had his arm around her."

Robin frowned. "Well, that's not a crime," she said, not convincing anyone.

Nikki knew Robin was only trying to cheer her up. She and Tim were history, and everyone must know it was over between them.

Lacey cast a worried look in her direction. "Maybe this is all a big misunderstanding. You still love Tim, don't you?"

"Well, how would *you* feel if you caught Rick with another girl?" Nikki asked. She turned to Robin. "Or if you found Cal with his arms around someone else? Would you put up with it?"

Robin nodded. "You've got a point. I'd probably strangle Cal first, and then her!"

Nikki sighed. "Well, every time I turn around, Tim's with Lara. Then he says it doesn't mean anything, that they're just friends."

"I still think you should talk to him," Lacey advised.

"No way!" Robin shook her head, and her long, dangling earrings jangled against her cheek. "Tim's the one who's fouled up. He should do the talking."

"He *has* tried to talk to me," Nikki admitted, feeling a little guilty. "But there's really nothing to say."

"Oh, Nikki," Lacey said softly, her light blue eyes clouding. "Maybe you should give him another chance. Tim's a great guy."

"*Was* great. Past tense," Nikki corrected. She took out her hairbrush and pulled it through her blond hair until it crackled; then she squared her shoulders.

Lacey bit her lower lip as she tried to tame her wavy red hair with a comb. "I just hope you're not making a big mistake, Nikki."

"I'm not," Nikki told her firmly. But she couldn't help feeling more than a little scared as she shoved the rest room door open and said goodbye to her friends. As she headed toward the north wing, she crossed her fingers and hoped she didn't run into Tim with Lara. *That* would be too much to take right then.

In the *Record* office Brittany Tate's fingers practically flew over the keyboard of the manual typewriter. Well, they would have flown if the *i* didn't keep sticking. She was behind deadline, as usual, but this was going to be one terrific column.

"Brittany?" DeeDee Smith, the editor-in-chief of the *Record,* poked her head over Brittany's shoulder. "About done?" she asked.

Brittany nodded. "In a minute."

"You're late," DeeDee reminded her.

"I know, but this article will be worth it, believe me," Brittany said, irritated. DeeDee could be a real slave driver, and Brittany didn't have a lot of extra time these days. She was still working a couple of evenings and some Saturdays as a waitress at Slim and Shorty's Good Eats Café to pay for her membership dues at the country club. No one but Jeremy and Kim knew about her job, however, and she planned to keep things that way.

"I can hardly wait to see the story," DeeDee said dryly.

"It's going to be great," Brittany promised. "Oh, I'll need someone to take a picture of the new French teacher. You know, the guy who's taking Madame Duval's place."

DeeDee looked skeptical. "I don't get it."

"I'm writing a series of short articles," Brittany explained. "Personality profiles to tag on to my regular column. For this issue, since I'm doing a follow-up on the play, I'll focus on Tim Cooper—"

DeeDee's brows pulled together over her brown eyes. She tapped her pencil against Brittany's desk. "But you just did a feature on Tim and Lara Bennett, remember?"

"I know, but this is different," Brittany insisted. "This new series will be about people in the school and how they affect life at River Heights High. It could be a student, a teacher, or even a well-known graduate."

"Like Nancy Drew," DeeDee said thoughtfully.

Brittany shuddered inwardly. Nancy Drew, the famous amateur detective, was Nikki Masters's good friend and next-door neighbor. Nancy had even worked on a case involving Nikki last summer. She had cleared Nikki of the murder of her boyfriend.

"Well, Nancy Drew is a possibility," Brittany said. Actually, she had no intention of doing any story that might remotely involve Nikki. "But Tim Cooper just started at River Heights High this year, and he's already played the lead in the school play. Now there's this new French teacher, Marc LeBlanc. I'm sure he'll change a few attitudes about foreign languages around here."

DeeDee crossed her arms over her chest and gazed at Brittany thoughtfully. "Okay, those are a few ideas. Any others?"

Brittany thought quickly. "Well, how about a story on Maggie Stark, the new star forward on the girls' soccer team?"

DeeDee seemed to be warming to the subject slowly. "Don't forget Emily Van Patten, the model," she added.

"Sure. Emily would be great," Brittany said without enthusiasm. She hated the little stab of jealousy she felt whenever Emily's name was mentioned.

DeeDee rubbed her chin. "Didn't she just finish a fashion spread for some big teen magazine?"

Brittany sighed. "I think so."

DeeDee's dark eyes twinkled. "And there are rumors that she's auditioning for a part on a new TV sitcom. You know, Brittany, this profile idea just might work."

"Thanks," Brittany replied with a grin. Compliments from DeeDee were rare. Brittany hoped to be appointed editor-in-chief of the paper for next year, and she'd need

DeeDee's support. "So, anyway," she went on, "I'll need a few pictures of Tim in the play."

"We've already got them," Karen Jacobs, the layout and production editor for the *Record,* called from the other side of the room. The girl had obviously been eavesdropping again. Karen was Brittany's main rival for the editorial job after DeeDee graduated.

Brittany managed a thin smile. "I'll also need shots of the new French teacher, Monsieur LeBlanc."

DeeDee turned to Karen. "Do we have anything on him?"

"Negative," Karen chirped. She rolled her chair into the center aisle between the desks. "I just checked. The guy didn't go to school here. There's nothing in the files." Karen took off her glasses and polished them on the hem of her sweater.

Brittany sighed. "Well, I'll need a couple of pictures to choose from for next week's edition."

"I'll let Nikki Masters know," DeeDee said. "She may want to shoot more pictures for us now that the play is over." She turned back to Karen. "What do we have on Emily Van Patten? We could use some shots of her at school and maybe something from her portfolio."

Karen looked flustered. "Well, I can look around, I guess."

"Are you kidding? We must have a million pictures of her," Brittany said.

"Sure," Karen said quickly, rolling her chair back to her desk.

What was that all about? Brittany wondered after DeeDee went back to her desk. Obviously Karen wasn't too crazy about Emily. But why? She certainly couldn't be jealous of the girl. Karen never seemed to care much about her appearance. She rarely wore makeup or bothered with her hair, and her clothes were always dull.

Brittany's eyes narrowed. Twice in the last week she'd seen Karen in the cafeteria with Ben Newhouse, the junior-class president. Good-looking and an A student, Ben was Mr. School Spirit with a capital *S*. He and Emily Van Patten were a serious couple. Was it possible that plain-Jane Karen had a secret crush on Ben? Brittany chewed on the tip of her pencil and filed that interesting possibility for future reference.

A few minutes later Brittany finished typing her column. She laid the finished pages on DeeDee's cluttered desk. DeeDee didn't even look up.

Scooping up her bag, Brittany set off for French class just as the bell rang. Students began pouring into the hallway. She touched her hair and checked to see that her short denim skirt was straight.

"Brittany! Wait up!"

Brittany turned to see Kim weaving toward her through the throng.

"It's crazy in here," Kim said in disgust as a short, freckled boy hurried by, nearly knocking her over.

"Sorry," he said quickly, flashing an apologetic and appreciative smile at her.

Kim rolled her eyes. "Freshmen! They're *all* geeks!"

Brittany said nothing. She was still thinking about her newspaper column.

"So where's Samantha?" Kim asked as they passed Samantha's locker.

"I haven't seen her since this morning before school," Brittany said with a shrug.

Kim raised her eyebrows. "I thought you two always walked to French together." She smiled slyly. "Maybe she's with her mystery man."

"Maybe," Brittany said. Obviously, Kim was put out because Samantha hadn't told her who the guy was.

Kim's steel blue eyes glinted a bit as they headed toward the north wing. "It's strange," she went on. "Samantha kept throwing me hints about this hot new guy, but I got the feeling she doesn't have a date for the dance on Friday."

Brittany gritted her teeth. She didn't have a date for Friday night, either. Ever since Westmoor University student Jack Reilly had broken up with her, she hadn't had many dates. She'd been so wrapped up in Jack that she hadn't been paying much attention to what was going on with the high school social scene. There wasn't really anyone who interested her at River Heights High, except Tim Cooper. As for the dance, maybe she could get Tim to ask her, now that Nikki was out of the way. She'd have to work fast, though. . . .

"There you are!" Jeremy Pratt caught up with Kim and Brittany as they rounded a corner. He dropped a casual arm around Kim's shoulders. "I thought we might go to the Pizza Palace after school."

"Are you driving?" Kim asked pointedly.

Jeremy's neck flushed. "Uh, yeah. The Porsche's running again."

Brittany smiled to herself. Jeremy had been a lowly dishwasher at the same café where she'd taken her lousy waitressing job. Jeremy had needed the money to fix his precious car, pay off gambling debts, and take Kim out in the extravagant style to which she was accustomed. Apparently, his angry parents had finally stopped paying his bills. Now, however, he no longer had to suffer the humiliation of working at a greasy burger joint. Kim had lent Jeremy the money to bail his car out.

Brittany sighed. She couldn't yet afford to give up her job, but she was looking forward to quitting in the very near future.

Right now, though, she didn't have any time to waste. She was anxious to meet the handsome Monsieur LeBlanc. And, of course, she'd be keeping a close eye on Samantha, too.

In all fairness, Brittany thought, it was high time that Samantha fell in love. But with a *teacher,* no matter how good-looking?

 **3**

Samantha slid into her seat and touched a hand to her hair for the thousandth time. Marc LeBlanc *had* to notice her!

She glanced up to see Brittany, cool as ever, making her way toward her desk just in front of Samantha's.

"Hi," Brittany said. She tossed her French text onto her desk and sat down. "I hope this new guy is an improvement over Madame Duval."

"I have a feeling he will be," Samantha replied, trying hard not to smile.

Monsieur LeBlanc strode into the room just as the final bell rang.

Samantha's heart flipped over.

Tall and lean, with jet-black hair and

flashing brown eyes, Marc was everything Samantha thought a Frenchman should be—handsome, sexy, and mysterious. He was wearing black corduroy pants and a black turtleneck.

Je t'aime, Samantha thought dreamily. That, she remembered, was the French phrase for "I love you." Or should she use the more formal address, *Je vous aime*? After all, they didn't know each other that well yet.

"Bonjour," he greeted the class. "I'm Monsieur LeBlanc. I'll be filling in for a few weeks until Madame Duval gets back on her feet. But you'll have to help me out. I'm going to have to refer to the class list for a couple of days until I get to know your names. So, please, stay in your assigned seats."

He smiled briefly in Samantha's direction, and she felt herself melt inside.

"Let's get started right away, shall we?" Monsieur LeBlanc continued.

The class groaned, but Samantha rested her chin on her palm, content to gaze at the teacher.

Monsieur LeBlanc rattled off something in French, and several students laughed at the joke, whatever it was. Samantha wasn't really listening.

"Okay, everyone, let's get down to business," he went on, leaning against the edge of his desk. "We'll start by reading aloud from the text. Page one hundred and sixteen." He reached for his own book and flipped it open. "Here we go—"

He had been looking straight at her. Samantha was sure of it. Her heart racing, she tilted her face up and smiled, ready to impress him with her flawless French.

"Nikki Masters, why don't you lead off?" Monsieur LeBlanc suggested.

Samantha's soaring spirits plummeted straight through the floor as Nikki started rattling off.

Samantha cast an unhappy glance in Nikki's direction.

No wonder Monsieur LeBlanc had noticed her. Nikki's blond hair shimmered, and her blue eyes had a warmth that even Samantha had to admire. The girl had everything—including, it seemed, the undivided attention of Monsieur LeBlanc. At least for now.

Samantha slid lower in her seat, wishing she could fade away as Nikki read on without stumbling once. No wonder Brittany was always trying to get the better of that girl, Samantha thought jealously.

"Perfect, Nikki! *Très bien!*" Monsieur LeBlanc said, training his sexy smile on a pleased-looking Nikki.

Samantha's stomach turned.

"Now, let's go on —" Monsieur LeBlanc said, consulting the class list. "Emily Van Patten?"

"She's not here today," Brittany piped up. "She's in New York City."

Monsieur LeBlanc's eyebrows elevated. "I see." He looked around. "Okay, so we need another volunteer." He searched his class list yet again. "Kyle Kirkwood, please read the next two pages."

Kyle, a tall boy in the front row, was a major brain. With his sandy hair, huge glasses, and lousy clothes sense, in fact, he took the cake for Geek of the Year, Samantha decided. Kyle ran his finger down the page and found his place. Then, with a lopsided grin, he started reading as effortlessly as Nikki had.

Great, Samantha thought.

Brittany turned and slipped a note onto Samantha's desk. Samantha pounced on the little piece of paper and unfolded it.

"Looks like N.M. has found another male admirer!!!" Brittany had written neatly.

Samantha's heart sank. Was it obvious to everyone?

Well, she could play the good little student just as well as Nikki. And if that's what it was going to take to get Monsieur

LeBlanc's attention, Samantha decided, she would just have to study harder. A *lot* harder, she added to herself.

Marc LeBlanc was definitely the most interesting male to pass through the corridors of River Heights High in ages. Samantha vowed silently that she would have him all to herself—even if it meant fighting Nikki and Brittany.

Brittany took her time leaving French class. Samantha would just have to wait for her. She gathered her books slowly and headed up to the teacher's desk. Then she delivered the handsome new substitute her most dazzling smile. *"Pardon, Monsieur LeBlanc."*

He grinned. "What can I do for you, uh"—he checked his class list—"Brittany?"

Annoyed that he'd had to look up her name, Brittany forged ahead. "I write for the school paper," she said breezily. "My column is called 'Off the Record.' I was hoping to do a short interview with you—a profile, actually—for next week's edition."

One side of Monsieur LeBlanc's mouth turned up. "I doubt a substitute teacher would be of any interest to your readers—" he began.

"Oh, no," Brittany rushed to assure him. Suddenly she sensed someone behind her. From the corner of her eye she caught Samantha heading slowly to the door. "I'm sure there are lots of people who'd want to know more about you," she went on quickly.

The teacher chuckled. "Well, if you really think so, it's okay with me."

Brittany beamed. "Great. I'll schedule a photo session and an interview——"

"Hold on a minute," Monsieur LeBlanc said, holding up one hand. "This is just a *short* piece, right?"

"Sure," Brittany assured him, "but we'll need a picture."

He nodded and stood up. "All right." With one finger he casually snagged his suit jacket from the back of his chair and hooked it over his shoulder.

"I'll let you know the time and place tomorrow," Brittany said.

Samantha was still lingering near the doorway as Brittany left the room. What was the matter with her? It wasn't like Samantha to be so shy. Brittany took her by the arm and led her out into the hall.

"What was that all about?" Samantha demanded.

Brittany nearly burst out laughing. The look on Samantha's face was positively murderous. "I just needed some material for my column," she said. "I'm doing a profile on Monsieur LeBlanc."

Samantha looked stricken, and Brittany felt a pang of remorse. After all, Samantha *was* her friend—even if she hadn't told her how she felt about Monsieur LeBlanc. If she wanted to keep her funny little secret, fine.

Samantha looked away. "Look, Brittany, I met Marc—that's his first name—over the weekend. I kind of thought—well . . ."

"You thought you'd get him to ask you out," Brittany finished.

Samantha blushed a little. "Well, yes."

The two of them stopped at Brittany's locker. "So, why didn't you tell me?" Brittany asked.

Samantha sighed. "Well, you and Kim have been pretty wrapped up in yourselves lately," she said defensively.

"Did I hear my name mentioned?" Kim asked, stepping through the crowd as Brittany twirled her combination lock. The girl had an amazing way of popping up and surprising people.

Brittany nodded. "Hi, Kim. Samantha was just explaining why she didn't let us know that she's fallen for the new French teacher."

Kim stopped dead in her tracks.

"Marc LeBlanc," Samantha said quickly. "I met him over the weekend, and he is *sooo* sexy!"

Brittany couldn't argue that point.

"But he's a *teacher*," Kim said, frowning.

Samantha shook her head. "I know, but he's also a graduate student at Westmoor."

"So, why didn't you tell us about this guy?" Kim asked, her blue eyes sharp.

Samantha hesitated.

"Come on, what's up?" Kim prodded. Brittany pawed furiously through her locker.

Taking a deep breath, Samantha said, "Ever since you started hanging around with Jeremy, Kim, you haven't had much time for your friends anymore."

Kim's mouth dropped open, but she snapped it shut quickly.

"And you," Samantha added, turning to Brittany. "All *you've* been able to think about lately is how to get Tim Cooper to dump Nikki Masters!

"Marc LeBlanc is the most amazing guy I've ever met," Samantha went on as the bell rang loudly. "And if I want to go out after him, I will. That's *my* business." She glared at her watch. "Look, guys, I'm late. I've got to run."

"Meet us after school," Kim called after her. "At the Pizza Palace!"

But Samantha was already halfway down the hall.

"I don't think she heard you," Brittany said, shaking her head as she watched Samantha disappear around the corner. "You know, I think we *have* neglected her lately."

"So? She has her own life to live." Kim was obviously put out.

Brittany slammed her locker door shut. It stuck and she gave it a slight kick. "I guess you're right. And right now, I have a feeling that life centers on Marc LeBlanc."

"In her dreams," Kim said, nodding to one of Jeremy's friends. "Listen, I've got to go, but we've definitely got to do something about Samantha. Falling for a teacher? The girl is crazy!"

"You haven't seen him yet," Brittany replied with a grin. She shrugged. "If I didn't have so much on my mind right now, I might be interested in the guy myself."

Kim's eyebrows nearly hit the ceiling.

"Only kidding," Brittany added quickly.

Nikki sagged against the locker next to hers. She had thought the horrible day would never end. She'd managed to make it through her classes without speaking to Tim. The classes she shared with him had been sheer torture. Whenever Tim had glanced at her, she'd forced a cool smile and looked right through him.

Nikki slipped the strap of her camera over her neck, trying to balance a huge stack of books as she reached to open her locker. Suddenly she came face-to-face with Lara Bennett.

Her heart sank.

"Nikki," the younger girl said, a troubled expression on her face. She swallowed hard. "I need to talk to you."

Nikki managed a nod. "Sure," she replied as casually as possible.

"It's about Tim."

Nikki froze. Would this girl never quit? "What about him?" she said aloud.

Lara fidgeted nervously, her green eyes avoiding Nikki's. "I—I think I've messed a lot of things up."

"What do you mean?" Nikki asked evenly. She wasn't going to give Lara any help.

"Well"—Lara shifted from one foot to the other—"I guess you know I like Tim. I like him a lot."

"So I noticed," Nikki said dryly.

"But I know you're going out with him,

and I didn't mean, um, I didn't want, well—oh, this is awful!" Lara was practically out of breath. "Tim *loves* you!"

"Loves me?" Nikki repeated, frowning. The scene between Lara and Tim at the cast party immediately flashed into her mind. "I don't think so."

"I didn't mean to break you two up!"

Lara was about ready to cry. Nikki couldn't help feeling regret for treating her so meanly. "Look, Lara," Nikki said, her voice surprisingly steady. "The trouble between Tim and me really doesn't have that much to do with you. If everything had been going well in the first place, then this whole thing probably wouldn't have mattered." She shrugged, trying to ignore her pain.

Lara blinked uncomprehendingly.

Nikki said, "The problem is between Tim and me, Lara. In fact, he should be the one talking to me about this, not you."

Lara hesitated. "I think he's tried."

Nikki tossed her hair away from her face. "He has, but I'm just not ready to talk to him yet."

"Maybe you should give him another chance," Lara said hopefully. Nikki could see that the girl was still suffering from a major crush on Tim. She knew it had taken a lot of courage for Lara to talk to her like this.

"I'll talk to him," Nikki said finally. "But I really don't think Tim and I will get back together again."

Lara brightened. "Well, I'll see you, Nikki," she said. "Thanks." She hustled down the hall just as Robin Fisher came up behind Nikki.

"What," Robin asked, eyeing the other girl with disapproval, "was *that* all about?"

Nikki sighed. "I think Lara was asking me to give Tim another chance. I guess she must be feeling a little guilty about the cast party. Not that it was all her fault," she added quickly.

Robin's eyes widened. "You're kidding! Did she apologize?"

"Well, kind of, I guess. But it doesn't matter," Nikki said.

"So it really is over?" Robin asked softly.

Nikki nodded, looking away. "It's over."

"Uh-oh," Robin said suddenly. "Here comes trouble."

Nikki glanced over her shoulder to see Brittany Tate heading straight toward them.

"Nikki! I've caught you," Brittany called, her black suede flats clicking down the hallway.

Nikki swallowed. What now?

Brittany gave Robin a quick nod, then zeroed in on Nikki. "DeeDee was wondering if you'd mind taking some pictures of Monsieur LeBlanc for the paper. Next week's edition, actually."

"For your column?" Nikki asked, raising her eyebrows slightly.

Brittany's smile faded a little. "I'm doing profiles of interesting people at River Heights High. You know, like a star of the week."

Nikki was still annoyed about the last piece Brittany had written, but how could she turn down a job for the *Record*? She *was* a staff photographer, she reminded herself.

"Tell DeeDee I'll try to get some candid shots of Monsieur LeBlanc during French class, okay?" she said finally.

Brittany seemed genuinely pleased. "That'd be great! And, listen, when Emily Van Patten gets back to school, we could use the same kind of shots. You know, pictures of her as a typical student."

"I'll try." Nikki gritted her teeth.

"Fantastic! This'll be the best series of

articles in ages." Brittany gave a little wave and took off down the hall.

"I wouldn't bet on that," Robin muttered. "But I do know one thing. When Brittany wants anyone to do anything for her, it's for one reason only—the good of Brittany Tate!"

 4

Ben Newhouse tossed his books into his backpack, slammed the door to his locker, and headed out of the school building. He felt guilty for canceling the junior class officers' meeting, but he just couldn't concentrate right then. Not when his girlfriend was finally flying back to River Heights!

Emily had been in New York for over a week. The two of them had talked on the phone almost every night, but for some reason their conversations were always strained. Ben couldn't shake the sinking feeling that something was wrong— something Emily wasn't telling him, or couldn't tell him.

Ignoring the noisy crowd of students spilling outside, Ben headed straight for the parking lot.

"Hey, Newhouse!" Rick Stratton called to him from the gym steps.

Ben paused, glancing at his watch. He didn't have much time, but Rick was a good guy.

"Lacey told me your meeting was canceled," Rick said, catching up with Ben. Rick's girlfriend, Lacey Dupree, was junior-class secretary. "If you're not busy, I thought maybe you'd be interested in a game of racquetball."

"Thanks, but I can't today," Ben replied. "I've got to pick Emily up at the airport right now."

Rick shoved a hand through his sandy hair. "So she's back from New York again?"

"She will be in an hour or so."

Rick walked Ben the rest of the way to the parking lot. "Lacey mentioned that Emily might be on the verge of becoming a major television star." He grinned. "Being a hot New York model isn't enough, I guess."

Ben's expression darkened.

"Hey, I didn't mean it that way," Rick said quickly. "Emily's a great girl."

Ben sighed. "Yeah, I know." He took

his car keys out of his pocket. "I did hear that she auditioned for a part on 'Three Strikes.'"

Rick stopped dead in his tracks and gave a low whistle. "'Three Strikes'? The new sitcom with that guy Jason Monroe?"

"That's the one." Ben's jaw tightened at the teen star's name. Jason Monroe's handsome face had been plastered over every glossy teen magazine in the racks lately. What bothered Ben most about the audition had nothing to do with Jason. It was the fact that Emily hadn't told him about it. He'd had to hear about it from her mother when he called New York the night before. That hurt. It didn't help that Emily had been out at the time, either. He'd spent ten minutes listening to her mother go on about Emily's rising career.

"I'd watch it if I were you," Rick teased good-naturedly as Ben climbed behind the wheel of his Toyota. "Jason Monroe is pretty heavy competition."

Don't I know it, Ben thought grimly. He glanced around the small car he'd once been so proud of. Jason Monroe probably drove a Ferrari or a Jaguar. He probably dated a different gorgeous girl every night, too. Maybe even Emily. Ben's hands tightened around the wheel.

"Don't even think about it," he told

himself, plunging his key into the ignition. The little car sparked to life. Ben gave Rick a wave as the Toyota roared out of the parking lot.

Once he hit the highway, Ben snapped on the radio, but he hardly heard the Dead Beats tune that filled the interior. He barely noticed the other cars vying for position on the interstate, either. All he could think about right then was Emily.

Why hadn't she told him about the audition? And why hadn't she called him back last night?

Ben pounded the steering wheel with his fist.

He knew that something was bothering Emily, and it was more than having to spend so much time in New York. Maybe it had something to do with this audition. Or maybe it had something to do with him. Maybe she wanted to break up.

Lost in thought, Ben nearly missed the turnoff for the airport. What was going on?

Emily yanked her suitcase from the baggage carousel, then grabbed her shoulder bag. With all the traveling she'd been doing lately, she had the airport routine down pat.

When she spotted Ben striding toward her, a big grin on his handsome face, she braced herself. The next hour or so was going to be rough. Very rough.

Her heart pumped a bit faster. Smiling, Emily gave Ben a wave. His dark hair gleamed and his brown eyes sparkled as he dashed across the baggage-claim area. "It's great to see you, Emily!" he said, swinging her off her feet. Then he kissed her long and hard on the lips.

"I missed you, too," she said, wincing. She still loved Ben, but things had changed. She only hoped he would understand.

"Did you?" As he set Emily back on her feet, he looked pleased. She wished she didn't have to hurt him.

The terminal doors opened automatically, and Ben led Emily through the parking garage to his little Toyota. Emily felt great sadness. Ben had first kissed her in that car, she remembered, feeling tears burn behind her eyes. Life had been so much simpler then. But now . . .

"Let's stop at the Pizza Palace on the way home," Ben suggested. "What do you say?"

"Why not?" Emily replied brightly. Maybe she would start feeling like a River Heights student again. Then she might be able to pretend for a while that everything wasn't falling apart.

Inside the car, she sat close to Ben, feeling his arm brush hers as he shifted into reverse and pulled out of the lot.

Emily could almost imagine what life would have been like if she hadn't gotten that first modeling job. If her mother hadn't insisted on packing her off to New York, if her father hadn't approved . . .

Ben draped his arm around her shoulders, and Emily smiled up at him. But soon, very soon, she was going to have to tell Ben the news.

Her throat grew hot as they sped down the highway. She closed her eyes and remembered how much she'd cared for Ben not all that long ago.

She didn't want to hurt him, but things were out of her control right now. Soon, she promised herself. I'll tell him soon.

Samantha tucked her purchases—two French magazines, a new shade of lipstick (advertised as *très chic*), and a pink silk blouse—into her oversize bag. Then she walked the few blocks to the Pizza Palace. She couldn't hang out long, though. She had to get home and hit the books as soon as possible.

As she pushed open the door of the Pizza Palace, the sound of music, laughter, and excited conversation greeted her.

She glanced around for Brittany and Kim just as Jeremy Pratt brushed past her balancing two large pizzas. "We were wondering if you'd make it," he said, indicating a corner booth with his blond head.

Samantha smiled and followed Jeremy to the booth where Kim, Brittany, and a couple of Jeremy's friends were sitting. She carefully avoided the gazes of Hal Evans and Wayne Yates, Jeremy's main sidekicks. Obviously, Samantha thought, Kim had to put up with Wayne and Hal because of Jeremy. But there was no reason on earth why she, Samantha Daley, had to be overly sociable with Jeremy's rich, stuck-up buddies.

"So where've you been?" Brittany asked as she reached for a small piece of pepperoni-and-olive pizza.

"Oh, shopping," Samantha replied airily.

"Already?" Kim looked at her in surprise. "Pretty fast work. School has only been out an hour."

"I just needed to pick up a few things," Samantha said vaguely. She wasn't about to go into detail about her purchases—not in front of the guys, anyway.

"So are you going to sit down or what?" Hal invited not very graciously.

Reluctantly Samantha took a seat next to

Hal, but he was the furthest thing from her mind. Since French class, she'd come up with a plan to get Marc LeBlanc's attention. Obviously, Marc had been impressed with Nikki Masters and Kyle Kirkwood in class that day. If good grades counted that much, Samantha decided, she'd have to turn her solid D average into an A-plus. Even if it meant she had to *study*.

She toyed with a piece of pizza and half-listened to the conversation. As usual, Brittany's gaze continuously drifted around the room. All of Kim's attention, it seemed, was on Jeremy.

Hal tried to make conversation with Samantha as he fiddled with the cheese shaker, but she was barely polite. He was *so* immature, just like all the other guys at River Heights High. *Not* like Marc LeBlanc.

"Well, well, well," Brittany said, eyeing the door. "Look who just breezed back into town."

Samantha followed Brittany's gaze. Ben Newhouse was walking Emily Van Patten to a small table for two.

"If it isn't River Heights's answer to Christie Brinkley," Kim said with obvious envy.

"I heard she tried out for a part in some

TV sitcom," Brittany said. "I wonder if it's true."

Kim shook her head. "Even if she did, it doesn't mean she'll get the part." She spiked an olive from her pizza with a fingernail.

But Brittany was watching Emily and Ben carefully. "Do you think there's trouble in paradise?" she asked.

Samantha glanced over at Ben and Emily's table. Ben's usual happy expression had faded, and he seemed to be speaking very seriously.

Emily looked nervous. She fingered her long blond hair and leaned back in her seat.

"No model-type smiles today," Jeremy agreed.

Brittany reached for her bag. "I think I'll just wander over and say hi," she announced.

"I'll join you," Kim said quickly. "Samantha?"

"I'd love to, but I really have to run," Samantha replied. "I've got tons of homework," she added.

"French?" Brittany asked, raising one dark eyebrow.

Samantha met Brittany's cool smile with one of her own. "That's right. I'll see you guys tomorrow at school."

"Count on it," Hal Evans said.

Samantha thought she might be sick. She wasn't interested in any of Jeremy's self-centered friends, least of all Mr. Ugly Evans.

With a wave, Samantha grabbed her things and headed out the door. She'd study French verbs all night if she had to, even if she had to ignore her chemistry assignment and prepare for tomorrow's history test. Right then she could only concentrate on one thing—Marc LeBlanc.

Glancing sideways, Emily saw Brittany Tate and Kim Bishop approaching their table. Inwardly she groaned.

She liked Brittany well enough. The girl could be pretty manipulative, but she was an interesting person. She could be fun, too.

Kim Bishop was another story. Emily didn't trust the snobbish, sharp-featured blond at all.

"Hi!" Brittany said as she and Kim reached the table. She flashed a big smile. "How was New York?"

Emily reminded herself to be very careful. She certainly didn't want to risk having anything she said end up in "Off the Record."

"Oh, New York was great," Emily said.

"Lots of jobs?" Kim asked pointedly.

"More than enough." What was it about Kim Bishop that immediately made her nervous? Emily wondered.

"I heard that you tried out for a part on a sitcom," Brittany said.

Emily nodded, swirling her straw in her diet soda. She wasn't about to lie to anyone, but she really wished she'd had the chance to talk it over with Ben first.

"Which one?" Brittany asked.

"'Three Strikes.'"

Kim's mouth fell open. "You're kidding!" she whispered. "With *Jason Monroe?*"

"I didn't read with Jason," Emily said with a shrug.

"But you met him?" Brittany cried.

Emily nodded. "Yeah, kind of."

"Did he talk to you?" Kim asked with obvious envy.

"Well, yes, a little."

"This is great!" Brittany said. "Listen, Emily, I'm doing a new series for 'Off the Record'—personality sketches, actually. I'd really like to do an interview with you the week after next. What do you think?"

Emily shifted uncomfortably in her chair. Ben was gazing at her silently. "Well, um, I don't know——"

"You don't have to go back to New York

again, do you?" Brittany asked. "I mean, you just got home."

Emily shrugged. "I'm just not sure, that's all. My schedule's kind of crazy."

Kim's eyes narrowed. "Too busy for everyone at River Heights High?" she asked, glancing at Ben.

Emily gulped. "Well, no, of course not. Sure, Brittany, I'll do the interview. But we'd better make it soon, okay?"

"Sure. I'll call you in a day or two," Brittany said, giving a little wave over her shoulder as she and Kim started back to their table.

Emily wanted to die. Ben was looking positively stricken. His troubled eyes searched her face.

"You're going back to New York again right away, aren't you?" he said finally. It was more a statement than a question.

She couldn't put off the inevitable any longer. "Yes." Emily swallowed the last of her drink, but her throat was still dry.

"When will you be back?" Ben seemed to be bracing himself for her answer.

She frowned and raised her eyes slowly to his. "I don't know, Ben," she said honestly. "Maybe never."

 5

Ben stared at Emily. "What do you mean, not coming back?" he said.

"It's real complicated," Emily said, glancing toward the booth where Brittany and Kim were sitting with Jeremy Pratt and his friends. Emily had a feeling they were all watching her.

"Try to uncomplicate it for me," Ben said bitterly. He drummed his fingers on the table. "Never mind. Don't tell me. Let me guess. You're too big a star for River Heights now, is that it?"

"No, but—" Emily began.

"But your career's too important for you to stick around here."

"Yes and no." Emily toyed with the salt and pepper shakers.

"Which is it?" Ben asked angrily, just as the number for their order was called over the loudspeaker.

He shoved his chair back and strode angrily over to the counter to pick up their pizza. Emily tried to think of the right words to explain things to Ben. Just tell him the truth, a voice inside her head demanded.

Ben returned, sliding the piping-hot mushroom-and-sausage pizza onto the table between them. "You know, Emily," he said, "I've really tried not to get too bent out of shape about your career. I mean, you should do what you want, and if you want to be a model . . ." He lifted his hand and let it fall to the table. "Well, okay. I guess that's what you should do. But I don't understand why you want to leave River Heights so much."

"I don't want to leave," Emily said, beginning to shred her napkin nervously.

"Then what is it?"

Emily glanced over at Brittany just as Brittany turned her eyes away. "Look, why don't we talk about this later—when we're alone?" she said.

Ben's jaw tightened, but he seemed to understand that they were being watched. "Okay," he agreed tersely.

Emily reached for a slice of pizza. How

was she ever going to tell Ben that they'd have to break up?

Nikki yanked her favorite pink leotard and purple spandex tights from her closet. She slipped them on and then popped a cassette into her tape player. Classical music began drifting from the speakers. Nikki hummed along, but her heart wasn't in it.

She propped her French book in front of her on the desk and started some stretching exercises as she read. Monsieur LeBlanc was giving them a quiz the next day. Nikki was pretty sure she knew the material cold, but it never hurt to review.

"Nikki!" Mrs. Masters's voice sounded above the music and broke her concentration.

Nikki snapped off the tape player as her mother poked her head into the bedroom. "Tim's downstairs, dear," Mrs. Masters said.

Nikki froze. "He's *here*?"

"He says he wants to talk to you."

Nikki almost told her mother that she didn't want to see him, but that would have been too childish. "I . . . I'll be right there," she said. Mrs. Masters nodded and headed back downstairs.

What would she say to Tim? Nikki

wiped a few drops of moisture from her forehead and glanced in the mirror. Her skin was flushed, and tendrils of blond hair had escaped from her ponytail to curl around her face. She was a mess.

It's now or never, Nikki decided finally, pulling on an oversize white sweatshirt. She spent a few seconds trying to deal with her hair, but it was hopeless.

She glanced down the stairs. Tim was in the entry hall, waiting.

Oh, please, Nikki thought desperately as she met his gray eyes, let me get through this without falling apart.

"Why don't we go outside?" she suggested. Her parents were around, and she didn't want them to overhear. She grabbed her black denim coat from the hall closet and headed out the side door. Tim was right behind her. He wasn't saying a word.

They crossed the frosty back lawn to an open gazebo not far from the pool. "We can talk in here," Nikki said. Her breath hung in foggy plumes as she exhaled.

"You've been avoiding me," Tim said flatly.

Nikki didn't answer.

"And you think I've been seeing Lara Bennett."

"It sure looked that way to me," Nikki said with a shrug.

Tim sighed and ran a hand through his hair. His shoulders were stiff, and his eyebrows met in an angry frown. "Why didn't you give me a chance to explain?"

Nikki steeled herself. "Because I was tired of arguing."

"But I love you."

That hurt. Nikki turned away. "I loved you too," she whispered.

"But not anymore?"

"I don't know," Nikki admitted. Tim reached up to touch her chin, gently moving her face back to meet his.

If only she could feel lighthearted and happy and in love again, she thought miserably.

Tim took her chilled fingers in his hands. A sudden warmth flooded through Nikki, but it wasn't the exhilarated, dizzy sensation she had felt in the past.

"I don't know what to say," Tim said, his voice rough.

"I . . . I don't either." Nikki silently prayed for strength. "But I think I need time—*we* need some time—apart."

"You want to break up," Tim said tonelessly.

"I don't *want* to, Tim. I just think we have to. Temporarily, I mean." Glad that she sounded more sure than she felt, Nikki withdrew her hands from Tim's and stuffed them into her pockets.

Tim's mouth stiffened into a thin white line. "I can't believe this is happening. Not to you and me, Nikki."

"I wish I could change things," she began. "But—"

"You know, I came to talk things over with you," Tim said harshly. "To talk about us. But I guess it isn't worth it, Nikki." He turned and started walking quickly away. "Just remember," he called over his shoulder, "breaking up was your idea!" With that, he strode across the frosted yard back toward the front driveway. He didn't look back.

Nikki dropped onto one of the benches and waited until she heard the sound of Tim's car starting in front of the house. That's it, she thought. It's really over. She was surprised to find that the pain was somewhat mixed with relief.

She drew her knees up, circling her legs with her arms as she stared at the covered pool. Yes, Nikki decided, it was time to start a new life—without Tim Cooper.

Karen Jacobs took off her glasses and rubbed her eyes. She'd worked late in the *Record* office, and it was nearly dark outside. But she'd done her job. She'd found several shots of Emily Van Patten for Brittany's upcoming article.

Frowning, Karen studied the glossy black-and-white photographs. There was no doubt about it, she thought ruefully. Emily was gorgeous. Even caught in candid shots, Emily's beauty shone through. And she was a nice person, too.

Karen picked up a photo of Emily taken the year before. It showed Emily working on the decorations for the Valentine's Day dance. Ben Newhouse was in the photo, too, leaning over Emily as they wound streamers together. Karen felt a tug at her heart.

How could she, Karen, ever have a chance with Ben? she wondered hopelessly. He was obviously in love with Emily. And why not? Emily was fun, vivacious, and totally beautiful. In some ways, Emily was a lot like Brittany Tate.

Karen sighed. Brittany had become her biggest rival for the editor-in-chief's job next year.

Brittany was a good reporter, all right. And people liked her—well, at least they acted as if they did. Brittany's smile was infectious, her energy seemingly endless, her popularity a fact of life at River Heights High.

Karen didn't trust the girl one bit,

though. Brittany was always stirring things up, poking her perfect nose in where it didn't belong.

Karen set the finished layout on DeeDee's desk, then noticed her reflection in a window backed by the dark night sky. No wonder Ben doesn't notice me, she thought miserably. She was so average looking. Totally boring.

Karen took off her glasses again, released her frizzy hair from its clip, and held it up away from her face. She turned her head from side to side, eyeing her reflection critically. Not much difference. She let her hair fall and clipped it back in its usual not-so-hot style.

She'd have to content herself with looking at Ben. One thing was for sure. She could *never* let Brittany get any idea of how she felt. Otherwise, Brittany would find a way to use that information against her.

Karen's gaze returned to the snapshot of Ben and Emily that was lying on her desk. Impulsively she picked up her scissors, cut Emily out of the picture, and tucked the small photo of Ben into her wallet.

Feeling a little better, Karen tossed the picture of Emily into the trash. There were other shots of Emily—plenty of them—that Brittany could use for her stupid article.

Karen left the remaining photographs on Brittany's desk, then slung her knapsack over her shoulder and headed out of the newsroom, locking the door behind her.

Someday, if she was patient enough and extremely lucky, she might get Ben Newhouse to realize that Emily wasn't the right girl for him. The right girl, Karen knew, was *her*.

Moon Lake had never looked more beautiful, Emily thought as Ben parked the car. Darkness had fallen, and frost clung to the edges of the lake. The water shimmered and sparkled, reflecting the stars overhead.

"Okay," Ben said, turning to Emily, "so what do you have to tell me?"

Emily swallowed hard. "I think we should start seeing other people."

"I knew it!" Ben said hotly, pounding his fist on the dashboard. "You just don't want to go out with me anymore."

"No, I . . ." Emily began.

"What?" Ben said, obviously wounded.

She closed her eyes. "Mom and I are moving to New York."

"So that you can be a big-time model and start a career in show business," Ben finished bitterly.

"It's more than that," Emily answered miserably, fighting the urge to cry.

Ben's eyes narrowed thoughtfully and his voice was softer. "Emily, what's wrong? Please tell me."

She felt the tears burning behind her eyes. "It's—it's my folks," she said unsteadily. "They're separating."

"What?" Ben frowned.

"They haven't decided to divorce yet. At least, that's what they're saying, but I think it's probably going to happen soon."

"But why?"

Emily shrugged and bit her lip. "They haven't gotten along for years. When I started modeling, my mom got real involved in my career."

Ben nodded. "That's for sure."

"But my dad thinks I should stay in River Heights and go to Westmoor University."

"Would that be so bad?" Ben asked.

Emily shook her head. "Of course not. But I can't give up my career now. It would kill my mom. And the way things are at home . . ." Her voice trailed away.

"So you think we have to break up."

Emily nodded, blinking back tears. "I think it would be best," she said, staring ahead through the partially fogged windshield. She tried to concentrate on the silvery waters of Moon Lake.

Ben folded his arms tightly. "Emily, tell me something. Have you been seeing anyone in New York?"

Emily felt like melting into the seat. "Yes," she answered softly.

"Who?"

"Nobody."

"Who?" Ben demanded. "Come on, I want the truth. You owe me that much."

Emily sighed. "I went out a couple of times with the son of a friend of my mom's. His name is Rory Chelton."

"Rory?" Ben repeated disbelievingly.

"It's nothing serious, Ben. I mean, I hardly know the guy."

Ben plowed a hand through his hair. Emily noticed that his fingers were shaking.

She touched his sleeve, but he drew away as if he'd been burned. "There's one more thing," she whispered. She might as well get everything off her chest at once.

"Oh, great. More good news," Ben said bitterly. "What is it?"

"I got a call-back for 'Three Strikes.'"

"So you'll be gone a long time."

Emily nodded. "Maybe. Look, I'm sorry things are working out this way for us."

"Me, too," Ben said, gazing out the windshield. "And I am sorry about your folks."

Emily felt a tear slide from the corner of her eye. She wiped it aside quickly. "Don't be sorry. There's nothing anyone can do."

Ben sighed. "So when do you go back to New York?"

She forced a wobbly smile. "At the end of this week. I just came back to pack a few things at the house and transfer my credits to a school in the city. I'm staying with my dad right now. My mom's waiting for me in New York." She swallowed hard. "Oh, Ben, we can still be friends."

"That doesn't usually work out," Ben said.

"I know," Emily said softly. "But I need a friend right now, Ben."

He took her in his arms and kissed the top of her head. "Okay, Em," he said. "But I'll always love you. Always."

6

Samantha finished the last question on the French quiz the next day and grinned. She'd aced it, she knew.

Nikki Masters and Kyle Kirkwood had both turned in their papers a few minutes earlier. But Monsieur LeBlanc had hardly seemed to notice.

Walking up to the front desk very slowly so that Marc would notice her sleek French braid, silky blouse, and short black skirt, Samantha handed in her quiz and flashed what she hoped was a brilliant smile in his direction. He glanced up at her with teacherlike interest, then went back to the papers he was already grading.

So much for wowing the guy with her new outfit.

Disappointed, Samantha returned to her seat. She pretended interest in her reading assignment, but she kept her eyes trained above the top of her book. She was happy just to drink in the sight of Marc LeBlanc.

She hardly noticed when Brittany got up to turn in her test paper, but she did see the note Brittany slid onto her desk. Samantha opened the folded scrap of paper and read, "Careful, you're drooling."

Blushing to the roots of her hair, Samantha tucked the note into her French book and cleared her throat. Had anyone noticed? She lifted her chin and returned to studying Marc a little less obviously. Brittany was just plain jealous! Aside from her fascination with Tim Cooper, Brittany wasn't interested in any particular guy at the moment. She probably couldn't stand to see anyone else in love.

After the last few students turned in their quizzes, Monsieur LeBlanc spent a few more minutes grading them. Just before the bell, he handed them back.

"*Très bon,*" he said to the class in general. "It seems like everyone studied last night."

You're not kidding, Samantha thought. She'd been up until one in the morning cramming French phrases into her brain.

Then she'd conjugated verbs until she couldn't prop her eyelids open another second.

Monsieur LeBlanc dropped Samantha's test paper onto her desk without so much as a smile. Had she blown it? But a big red *A* was scratched in the top right corner. She scanned both pages. She hadn't missed one question!

The bell rang and everyone started reaching for books and backpacks. Monsieur LeBlanc held up his hand. "We'll be having another quiz on Friday. Please read the following pages for tomorrow —" He rattled off the assignment and Samantha scribbled it down carefully in her notebook. Her heart sank when she couldn't even catch Marc's eye. Didn't he realize how hard she worked? She'd gotten an A, for heaven's sake.

To her mortification, Samantha watched as Nikki asked a couple of questions in perfect French. A crooked grin slashed across the teacher's face as he listened.

Nikki must have said something extremely witty, because Marc laughed, a deep, rumbling chuckle. If only *she* could make him laugh like that!

Kim was waiting for Samantha and Brittany at the door. "Well, I see Nikki Masters is back to charming every male in River Heights," she said sarcastically as they came out.

Inside the classroom, Nikki and the teacher were still rambling on in French.

"Mmm," Brittany said with a sidelong glance at Kim. "What do you suppose they're talking about?"

"Probably tomorrow's assignment," Samantha replied sharply.

Kim smiled at Brittany. "Of course," she said dryly.

The three of them stopped at Kim's locker and Brittany touched Samantha on the shoulder. "Don't you think it might be a good idea if you gave up on Monsieur LeBlanc?"

"Why should I?" Samantha asked.

"Because the whole idea's crazy, that's why," Kim said, joining in. Her gold bracelets jangled as she tried to juggle her books and open her locker at the same time.

Brittany nodded. "No way is a guy like that going to fall for a student."

"You don't know that," Samantha said.

"Oh, Samantha, get real," Kim said, rolling her eyes. "Even if he *was* interested in you, there are rules against things like that. He could lose his job, for one thing."

Samantha couldn't believe her ears. Kim and Brittany were her two best friends in the world. Why would they be saying such horrible things? Unless, of course, they were jealous, she reminded herself.

"I've told you a million times," Kim said, "you should try dating one of Jeremy's friends. Hal Evans really isn't so bad once you get to know him."

"I've told *you* a million times, I can't stand Hal!" Samantha snapped.

Kim's mouth clamped shut. "I was just trying to help."

"Maybe I don't need any help," Samantha tossed back in her low southern drawl. "In fact, I'll thank you both to mind your own business. I am perfectly capable of handling my own love life."

She turned on her heel and stormed off to her next class, leaving Kim and Brittany standing openmouthed in the middle of the hall.

At the end of the day Brittany was still thinking about Samantha's outburst. The poor girl was really off the deep end over Monsieur LeBlanc. Sure, the guy was good-looking and sexy, but he was a *teacher*, for heaven's sake!

Walking briskly toward the *Record* office,

Brittany caught sight of Ben Newhouse coming out of chemistry lab.

Brittany hurried to catch up with him. "Ben!" she called. "Hey, wait up!"

Ben tried to smile when he saw her, but he wasn't entirely successful. Something was definitely going on, and Brittany suspected it had to do with Emily Van Patten.

"Hi, Brittany," he said. "What's up?"

"You tell *me,"* Brittany replied, unable to resist a little flirting. "Actually, I was hoping to run into you."

Ben raised his eyebrows. "Oh, yeah?"

Brittany gestured to several posters tacked up on the wall behind him. "Well, I remembered that you're in charge of Winter Carnival this year."

"Yes, unfortunately." Ben sighed as they headed toward the north wing. "We've all been going crazy trying to get everything coordinated."

"Well, I thought maybe I could help out with some of the last-minute details." Brittany had to half-run to keep up with Ben's long strides.

"Great," he said, nodding. "We could use you in decorations or donations."

Neither of those tasks sounded very appealing. "What about publicity?" Brittany asked quickly. "I mean, I *do* work on the paper."

"Karen Jacobs already said she'd handle that," Ben said. "What we really need is someone with a talent for collecting money. How about it?"

Brittany wasn't exactly thrilled about the idea of begging for money. "I could give the decorating committee a hand," she suggested. Before Ben could answer, she added quickly, "I know Emily's in charge of decorations, but she's out of town so much, she could probably use the help."

Ben's expression darkened. "Emily's not working on Winter Carnival anymore."

"Why not?" Brittany asked, raising her eyebrows.

"She had to back out because she won't be around," Ben said. "And if I were you," he added, "I wouldn't be planning any big articles about her in the *Record*."

"I don't understand—" Brittany began.

"Believe me, neither do I," Ben muttered as he spied Rick Stratton. "Look, Brittany, I've got to run. I'll put you down on the decorating committee, okay? Thanks a lot!" With that, he jogged down the hall to meet Rick.

Brittany was left with a thousand more questions about Emily—*and* now she was going to have to work on one of Ben's committees.

Brittany finally reached the *Record* office. She shoved open the door of the newsroom. Inside, students were working feverishly, putting the final touches on the next edition.

Brittany slid into her chair and spotted her final draft of "Off the Record" lying on top of her typewriter. "What's this?" she asked no one in particular as the editor-in-chief approached.

"I thought your column needed a little more work," DeeDee said with a shrug. She pointed to a few red marks on Brittany's perfectly typed page.

Brittany was offended. "What do you mean?"

"It's not exactly your best effort, Brittany," DeeDee replied. "I think the story on the play needs a little fleshing out. Maybe you should talk to some of the other kids who were in *Our Town*. We need other perspectives besides Tim Cooper's." She tapped the eraser end of her pencil against her cheek. "Maybe you should start with the drama teacher or Nikki Masters. After all, Nikki did play the female lead."

"I tried—" Brittany started to protest, but shut her mouth quickly. She was professional enough not to come up with lame excuses. Besides, she had part of an interview with Nikki. Now, where was it? With a sinking heart she realized she'd thrown her notes away. "I'll get right on it," she told DeeDee with a sigh.

Once the editor-in-chief had walked back to her desk, Brittany headed to the large wastebasket near the door. Good, it hadn't been emptied the night before. Then, as casually as possible, she pulled it back to her desk. Fortunately, everyone seemed too busy to notice.

Brittany rummaged carefully through the trash, not wanting to get any ink on her hands. She pulled out anything that looked remotely like the notes she'd thrown out the day before.

As she unfolded one piece of crumpled paper after another, a black-and-white photograph fluttered to the floor. Brittany was about to toss it back in the basket when she noticed that the glossy had been chopped up—but not professionally cropped. What was this? she wondered, recognizing a picture of Emily Van Patten.

In the photo Emily was twisting streamers for last year's Valentine's Day dance.

Interesting, Brittany thought. She pawed through the rest of the trash and finally discovered her notes at the very bottom of the basket. She smoothed them out and found a couple of boring quotes from Nikki. Then, glancing nervously at the clock, she rewrote her entire story.

"That should do it," she said, relieved to have made her deadline. She had to work at Slim and Shorty's that night, and she didn't have any more time. As she picked up her bag, Brittany noticed a pile of photos on the corner of her desk. Riffling through the stack of black-and-whites, she saw that the shots were all of Emily Van Patten. Karen Jacobs, Brittany had to admit, did quick work.

Then Brittany's eyes narrowed. Had Karen cut up the picture of Emily she had found earlier? If so, why? Practical Karen hardly seemed the type to sit around mutilating old photos.

Brittany studied the cut-up snapshot again and frowned thoughtfully.

Who or what had been cut from the picture? There was only one logical answer.

Slowly Brittany began to smile. She carefully tucked the damaged photo into her bag for safekeeping. It was possible she might need it—sometime.

The next two days were extremely difficult for Samantha. She spent almost all of her free time studying French. During study hall, which she usually spent gossiping with Kim, she wrote French essays. After school, instead of shopping or meeting friends, she went directly home and memorized zillions of useless French phrases. After dinner she hit the books again until long after midnight. Practically the only thing she'd done besides study lately was make up with Kim and Brittany for the stupid argument they'd had.

Now, getting ready for school on Friday morning, she yawned, feeling a tiny twinge of guilt that she'd neglected her other classes. She knew in her heart, however, that a few bad grades would be worth the prize: Marc LeBlanc.

Samantha checked her reflection in the mirror one last time. Her new lipstick, Paris Plum, matched her earrings. She placed a black beret jauntily on her head and smiled smugly.

"If that doesn't look French, I don't know what does," she said, admiring her striped black-and-purple turtleneck and matching purple skirt. Stifling another yawn, she scooped up her books and rushed downstairs to the kitchen, where her mother was making breakfast.

"Don't bother with anything for me," she said as Mrs. Daley, who was an older version of her daughter, looked up from the waffle iron. "I'm late already."

"But, Samantha——" Mrs. Daley began in her thick drawl.

"Really, I'm fine," Samantha said quickly. "And I don't need another lecture on 'Breakfast: The Most Important Meal of the Day'!"

Her mother sighed and shook her head. "No lectures this morning, Samantha. I don't have time. But eat *something,* please."

Just then a car horn blasted outside. Samantha snatched an orange from a bowl on the table and waved it under her mother's nose. "Wholesome, natural, and filled with vitamin C."

Her mother laughed as the horn sounded again.

Samantha headed for the door. "That's Kim. I'd better go."

Waving to her mom, she dashed outside into the crisp morning air. Gray clouds covered the sky. In spite of the cold, which she generally didn't like, Samantha felt wonderful. She was certain she'd finally make some progress with Marc that day.

"Good morning," Samantha chirped as she climbed into Kim's car.

"What's so good about it?" Kim asked grumpily. "Besides being Friday, I mean."

Samantha sighed happily. "Everything!"

"You're beginning to sound as dippy as Lacey Dupree," Kim told her. She glanced at Samantha, then twisted to look out the rear window as she backed out of the driveway.

"Thanks a lot!" Samantha said. Unwilling to let Kim's sharp tongue ruin her good mood, she began to peel her orange, tossing the peels out of the car window.

"This wouldn't have anything to do with a certain Monsieur LeBlanc, would it?" Kim asked suspiciously.

"Mmm." Samantha, not wanting to get into another argument with Kim about Marc, tried to sound noncommittal.

"Samantha, I'm telling you, he doesn't even know you're alive."

"Of course he does," Samantha said, facing Kim. But her friend didn't seem to be needling her, really. In fact, Kim's expression was concerned.

Samantha sighed and snapped on the radio. The weather report was predicting an early frost and cold, possibly snow. "Perfect," she cooed, popping an orange section into her mouth. "A record early snow."

"You know, Samantha, I don't mean to go on and on about this, but I'm really starting to worry about you," Kim said. A familiar Dead Beats song began filtering through the speakers.

Samantha widened her eyes. "Why?"

"You're taking this Monsieur LeBlanc thing too far, that's all."

"You don't know what you're talking about," Samantha said, staring straight ahead.

"I *do,*" Kim insisted. "Think about Brittany and all the trouble she had with Jack Reilly."

Samantha shrugged. "So?"

"Well," Kim said, sliding a glance in Samantha's direction, "for one thing, Jack was only a college student. Monsieur LeBlanc is even older than he is."

Samantha smiled. "Age doesn't matter, Kim. Not if you're in love."

"Oh, for heaven's sake," Kim said in disgust. "Get real." She shook her head as they pulled into the school parking lot. "You've got it bad."

"I know what I'm doing," Samantha insisted.

"I sure hope so." Kim guided her car into the parking spot closest to the school building. Jeremy was waiting for her near the back doors as usual. She quickly checked the rearview mirror to make sure that her makeup was perfect.

As Samantha reached for the car door, Kim touched her on the shoulder. "Wait, Samantha. Not so fast."

"What now?" Samantha said irritably.

Kim sighed. "Look, I know Marc LeBlanc isn't taking you to the dance tonight, so why don't you double with Jeremy and me? If Hal is too repulsive, think about Wayne Yates. I don't think he's got a date."

Samantha shook her head. "No, thanks. If I can't go with Marc, then I'd rather not go at all."

"Suit yourself." Kim pulled the key from the ignition and tossed the key ring into her oversize designer bag. "Good luck," she said, but she didn't sound as if she meant it.

Samantha climbed out of the car and adjusted her beret. The whole weekend stretched in front of her. And with a little luck, she might be spending at least part of it with Marc LeBlanc!

7

"Great job," Monsieur LeBlanc said, handing Nikki's essay back to her on Friday afternoon.

Samantha positively steamed. She'd gotten an A on *her* essay, too, but Marc had chosen Nikki's to read aloud.

Nikki smiled up at Monsieur LeBlanc. For the first time, Samantha realized that all her work had been for nothing. Every time she'd gotten a perfect score on a quiz, Marc handed back her paper with the same smile he'd given every other person in the class.

No, good grades obviously weren't going to do the trick.

Samantha chewed on one glossy fingernail before catching herself. She was ruining the new plum polish the salesgirl had insisted was so chic. Well, Samantha thought dismally, it might be the rage in Paris, but in River Heights it wasn't being noticed by a certain French-American. Brittany had done a little research on Marc and found out that only his father was French.

"Okay, class," Monsieur LeBlanc said as the final bell clanged, "don't forget to study this weekend!"

The class let out a collective groan.

Marc grinned. "I'm just reminding you that next week we're having a test. As you know, it will be worth three quiz grades."

Students started shuffling out of the room, but Monsieur LeBlanc wasn't finished. "I need someone . . ."

Samantha beamed in his direction, but his gaze landed on Nikki.

"Nikki, would you mind bringing in a copy of Hugo's *Les Misérables*—the French edition—sometime next week? I think you'll find it in the library."

Nikki gave the teacher her perfect Nikki smile. "I have it at home, I think."

He smiled back. "Terrific."

Samantha lingered for a moment, gazing at Monsieur LeBlanc. He didn't so much as look up when she passed his desk. Dejectedly she continued to the hallway.

Brittany was waiting for her outside the door. "You don't give up, do you?" She grinned at her friend. "You know Nikki and Tim broke up. It's official. So if you really want to get Monsieur LeBlanc to notice you, you'd better work fast. Who knows what Miss Have-It-All Masters has up her sleeve?"

Brittany was only kidding, of course, but still . . .

"I have got a plan," Samantha replied coldly.

Brittany's brows lifted. "What kind of plan? If it's all the extra studying you've been doing, forget it. It's not working."

She was right, and Samantha knew it. But another plan was beginning to form in her mind. A pretty daring plan. Samantha bit her lip.

"Being a superstar in French is no big deal," Brittany continued. "You've got too much competition from Nikki and that nerd Kyle Kirkwood."

That was why her new plan would be perfect, Samantha thought. "Oh, I know," she said aloud. "Don't worry. By the end of next week, things will be completely different."

"If you say so," Brittany replied dubiously, watching Samantha hurry off to her next class. She only hoped her friend knew what she was doing.

She couldn't worry about Samantha right then, though. She had to track down Emily Van Patten. She hadn't shown up for French again, and Brittany had heard a rumor that Emily was leaving River Heights for good. Also, Ben had been acting very strangely for a few days.

Brittany had other things on her mind, too. She didn't have a date for the dance that night, not to mention Jeremy's party in two weeks. Ordinarily Brittany might have passed up the events, but her social life had been deteriorating lately. She was working too hard to get together her money for her country club dues.

Forget Emily, Brittany decided. It was more important right then for her to find Tim Cooper. . . .

Glancing at the hall clock, Karen Jacobs rounded a corner on her way to chemistry and nearly bumped into Ben Newhouse. She managed to skid to a stop just before they actually collided, but she felt like a total fool anyway. "Oh, I'm—um, sorry," she said as Ben caught her elbow in his hand. She knew that her face was beet red.

"It's okay," Ben assured her. His dark

eyes were kind. "I guess I wasn't looking where I was going."

"Me, neither," Karen said quickly.

"Besides," Ben added, "I need to talk to you."

"You do?" Karen said, dumbfounded. What could Ben possibly want? She forgot all about the lab work she had to finish in chemistry as her heart started to pound crazily. Maybe he was going to ask her to the dance! But what about Emily?

"Yeah. I'm still a couple of volunteers short for Winter Carnival." Ben flashed Karen his megawatt smile.

"Oh." Her spirits nosedived. Of course. He wanted her to help with a project. It was nothing personal. How could she have thought anything like that, anyway? "Well, sure, I'd be happy to help. What's left?"

"I need someone to head up the donation committee," Ben answered. "I know you've already promised to work on publicity, and collecting donations is a lousy job, but—" He gestured helplessly.

"I'll do it," Karen said immediately.

Ben's face lit up. "You will? That'd be great!"

"Anything else?" Karen was desperate to keep the conversation going.

"That's more than enough," Ben said with a chuckle.

"You're sure?" Karen persisted. Any time she spent on the carnival would be spent, in part, with Ben.

Ben grinned. "Positive. Don't forget our general meeting on Monday. It's after school in the civics room."

"I'll be there," Karen promised.

"Terrific!" Ben replied, but his smile fell as he looked over Karen's shoulder.

Karen turned.

Emily Van Patten, carrying several heavy-looking book bags, was heading their way. Her glossy lips were set in a grim line, and her perfectly shaped eyebrows were drawn into a frown. Karen's heart sank.

"I'll catch you later, Karen," Ben said, taking off toward Emily.

"Sure." Karen suddenly felt invisible as she took in Emily's shining blond hair, black stretch pants, and oversize sweater.

She glanced down at her own outfit— jeans and a navy blue crewneck sweater. Not exactly sexy. In fact, it was downright boring. Maybe she could try a little harder to do something about her looks. After all, she was probably going to see a lot of Ben next week. And according to the latest rumor, Ben and Emily had actually broken up. But with the sappy way Ben was looking at Emily right then, Karen doubted that rumor very much. Karen averted her gaze as Ben and Emily began talking together.

She leaned against a bank of lockers and blew her bangs out of her eyes. Could she actually change her image? Lara Bennett had certainly improved her appearance after hanging around Brittany Tate for a while. But become glamorous overnight? Even if she did, would Ben notice?

By now the halls were completely empty, Karen realized. She was very late for chemistry. She turned and hazarded one last glance at Ben and Emily. They seemed to be talking rapidly, both their faces cold and set. For a couple who had so recently been in love, they acted as if they were definitely having problems.

Karen's heart lifted a little; then she was instantly ashamed of herself.

Oh, stop it, she told herself. You're starting to think like Brittany Tate! And that, she knew, could only spell trouble.

After school Brittany plowed through the wet, slushy snow on her way to Kim's car. Her boots began to leak, and her toes felt frozen stiff by the time Kim unlocked the door.

Shoving her hair back from her face, Brittany slid gingerly into the passenger seat.

Kim arched one brow. "Bad day?"

"It could've been worse," Brittany said, though she didn't see how. She'd spent most of the afternoon between classes trying to find Tim Cooper, and she hadn't seen him once. She'd even staked out his locker—inconspicuously, of course. She definitely had no date for the dance now.

Kim pointed through the windshield. "There's Samantha. I offered her a ride home, but she wasn't interested." She frowned. "I wonder what she's up to."

Brittany was too cold to care. "I wouldn't worry about it," she said, fiddling with the dial on the radio as Kim pulled the car out of the lot. One of Brittany's favorite songs filled the interior of the car, and she leaned back against the seat.

Kim glanced at Brittany. "So, have you decided about going to the dance?" she asked casually, turning down the main street and eyeing the window of a fashionable boutique.

"Mmmm," Brittany replied. "Maybe. Are you and Jeremy still planning to go?"

Kim laughed and cranked hard on the wheel, pulling into the parking lot of Leon's, one of their favorite hangouts. "Jeremy thinks the dance will be a drag, but we'll probably check it out after we have dinner at the country club. If the music's good, we'll stay, but if the dance turns into a geekathon, we'll leave."

"And go where?" Brittany asked without much interest.

Kim shrugged. "Oh, I don't know. Maybe to Commotion. Come on, let's get a soda and see who's here."

They started toward the front door, and Brittany had to stomp her boots twice on the way.

Leon's was extremely crowded. Kids were clustered around tables, munching fries and onion rings or nibbling on nachos. A few couples danced near the blaring jukebox, and others were hanging out near the counter.

Kim and Brittany found a booth where they could comfortably check out the action.

A plump waitress with flaming red hair walked over to their table. "What'll it be?" she asked in a bored voice.

"Diet soda and fries," Brittany replied.

"I'll have the same." Kim waited for the woman to disappear. "So, how's Samantha doing?" she asked. "I didn't see her much today."

Brittany shrugged. "She's still head-over-heels in love with Marc LeBlanc, I guess."

Kim snorted. "She's crazy," she said, drumming on the table with her fingers. "I told her so, too."

Brittany was beginning to grow bored with the whole Samantha situation. If the girl wanted to fall for a teacher, fine. She'd already told Samantha what she thought. It wouldn't be Brittany's fault if Samantha ignored her perfectly good advice.

Brittany knew most of the other kids in Leon's. She also knew that a lot of them were glancing her way—the boys admiringly and the girls enviously. She loved the attention, but the only person she really wanted to admire her was Tim. She hadn't gotten very far with him—yet.

If only her plan to snare Tim at the beginning of the school year hadn't backfired so badly. Nikki Masters had gotten in the way, as usual. . . .

The waitress deposited their drinks and fries on the table without a word, then snapped her order book open and headed for the next table.

Kim dipped a french fry in a small pool of catsup. "I just don't think Samantha should bother trying to get a teacher to notice her," Kim said thoughtfully.

Brittany was startled from her thoughts. "Maybe Samantha will get interested in someone else," she said with a shrug.

"But who?" Kim asked. "Lots of guys ask her out, but she just isn't interested. And I'm sure I could fix her up with someone."

"I know, but Samantha's too proud to be fixed up," Brittany said, swirling her drink with her straw and studying the ice cubes as they clinked together. "But maybe we could help her along. You know, introduce her to some new guys without being too obvious." She leaned forward. "You know, Ben Newhouse is free."

"But he's crazy about Emily," Kim said.

"Was," Brittany corrected. "Past tense. They're history."

Kim frowned. "Are you sure?"

"Positive. In fact, Emily backed out of an interview with me because she won't be in River Heights much longer!" Brittany grinned at Kim's wide-eyed surprise. "So that leaves Ben very unattached."

"I'll bet he's not over Emily, though," Kim pointed out. "I'm telling you, the guy was madly in love with her."

Brittany's eyes twinkled. "Maybe Samantha could help him forget Emily."

"I don't know. Ben's so involved in Student Council and all those activities. I mean, he practically runs River Heights High. He might be too rah-rah for Samantha."

"Well, maybe," Brittany said, but the wheels were already turning in her mind.

Samantha walked back into the school building, hoping to thaw her frozen fingers. Where *was* Marc LeBlanc, anyway? She'd hung around the faculty parking lot for nearly an hour, hoping to catch a glimpse of him.

Ready to give up, Samantha walked back out of the school wishing she'd taken Kim up on her offer of a ride. Then she saw him. His dark head bent against the wind, Marc was half-running across the faculty parking lot.

Samantha didn't waste a second. She hurried after him, waving furiously. "Monsieur LeBlanc!"

Marc stopped beside his car. His face was flushed from the cold. "Oh, hi, Samantha," he said, pulling his keys out of his pocket and unlocking the driver's door. "What're you doing here so late? I thought everyone tore out of school the minute the last bell rang."

"Well, um, I usually do," Samantha said

quickly. "But I was studying in the library and then I had trouble with the combination on my locker, and by the time I got out of the north wing my ride was gone and the buses had taken off." Breathless and nervous, she could hear her southern accent getting stronger and stronger. "Actually, I was hoping I could find someone to give me a lift home. . . ."

Marc checked his watch and frowned. "Well, I'm already late for a class at Westmoor. Maybe someone else . . ."

Samantha's heart turned cold. She felt like a total fool. "Oh, sure." How was she going to get out of this gracefully?

"Hey, there's Kyle," Marc said, pointing over Samantha's shoulder. "Hey, Kyle, over here!"

Samantha wanted to die. Cringing, she prayed that Marc wasn't talking about geeky Kyle Kirkwood. She turned slowly, and sure enough, it was Kyle in a huge winter jacket, boots, and bright green ski cap, slogging through the slush.

Samantha shuddered. "It's all right, really," she said hastily. "I'm sure I can find someone who——"

"What's going on?" Kyle nearly slid into them.

"How would you like to rescue a damsel

in distress?" Marc asked, clapping him on the shoulder. "Samantha here missed her ride home."

Samantha held up her hand. "No, really. I'll be fine."

"No problem." Kyle smiled at her. He did have a nice dimple, Samantha noticed. He was hardly her type, though—more like a guy for Karen Jacobs.

Marc reached for the door handle. "Look, Samantha, I'd feel better knowing that you weren't out here freezing to death." He smiled at her. "Any other time, I'd be happy to take you home. It's just lucky Kyle showed up when he did."

That's what *you* think, Samantha thought darkly. "I could walk—" she began.

"And I'd feel like a louse," Marc told her. "Kyle will be happy to give you a ride, I'm sure."

Kyle nodded, grinning.

There was no way out of this, Samantha thought.

"Well, I guess it would be all right," she said, casting an unsure glance at Kyle. What if someone saw her in a car with one of the biggest geeks in the school? Thank goodness Kim and Brittany were long gone.

"Look, I've really got to run," Marc said. He smiled at Kyle. "Make sure she gets home safely."

"I will," Kyle promised as Marc climbed into his car and started the engine.

With a horrible sinking feeling, Samantha watched him drive out of the lot.

"Well, let's go," Kyle said, heading toward an old pickup splotched with primer paint.

Samantha hesitated.

"Oh, come on, Samantha. Just get into the truck, okay?" Kyle said, opening the door. He looked at Samantha in disgust. "Don't worry. No one will see you."

Samantha cringed. She couldn't tell from Kyle's expression whether he was hurt or angry. "It's not that—" she said, climbing into the truck.

"Sure." Kyle slammed the door closed, and Samantha slid low in the passenger seat. This afternoon certainly wasn't turning out the way she'd planned.

Brittany was growing bored at Leon's. No one very exciting had shown up. She reached for her coat just as a blast of cold air blew into the room. Tim Cooper was walking through the door, his face ruddy from the cold. Brittany's heart turned over as Tim took a seat on the other side of the restaurant and the plump waitress scurried his way.

"Well, well, look who's here all by himself," Kim said with a smirk.

"I think I'll go over and say hi," Brittany said quickly, sliding out of the booth.

Kim rolled her eyes. "I wish you'd give up on this whole Tim thing, Brittany," she said. "You're as bad as Samantha."

Brittany pretended not to hear.

Tim glanced up as she approached. "Don't tell me," he said, smiling weakly. "Another article for the paper."

"Oh, no." Brittany sat down in the chair across from him. "Actually, I thought you might want to join Kim and me. Unless you're waiting for someone."

"No one in particular," Tim replied, and pinched his lips together. Brittany realized with a jolt that he was hoping to see Nikki.

Brittany's spirits nosedived. So he was still pining over Miss Have-It-All Masters. Well, she'd just have to change all that. "Come on," she said, inviting him again. "We're dying for some company. Really."

"Well, okay." Tim nodded to the waitress and followed Brittany back to her booth. Kim had her compact open, checking her lipstick.

"So, what're you doing this weekend,

Tim?" Kim asked, snapping the compact closed. "Any big plans?" Brittany slid into the seat next to Tim.

He shrugged. "Oh, I don't know—maybe I'll go to the dance. I haven't really made any plans."

Kim glanced quickly at Brittany and then back to Tim. "Well, Jeremy and I are going to the club, but we're planning to check out the dance later. What about you, Brittany?"

"I, uh, haven't decided," Brittany said. She threw a horrified look in Kim's direction. What did her friend think she was doing?

"We could all go over to Commotion if the dance isn't that great," Kim went on. Brittany tried to poke Kim's shin with the toe of her boot.

For the first time Tim looked as if he understood. The back of his neck flushed a bit, and Brittany wished she could melt right into the cushions of the booth.

"Sure," he said finally. "I guess that would be okay."

"Brittany?" asked Kim blithely.

Brittany's teeth were clamped shut. "I'll be there," she said barely audibly. Deep in her heart, of course, she wanted to be with Tim, but she didn't need Kim manipulat-

ing him into taking her out. Brittany pre-
ferred the date to be Tim's idea—or even
better, hers.

The three of them made small talk,
and Tim kept shooting glances at the
door. When he finished his soda, he
nearly bolted from his seat. "I'd better get
going," he said. But his hand rested for a
moment on Brittany's shoulder. "I'll see
you later," he said, and her pulse
kicked into double time. Lost in his
gray gaze, she didn't even see Nikki
Masters. She was standing just inside
the door.

Tim started away from the booth and
stopped, his face white. Nikki nodded
at Tim, then looked past him at Brittany.
Her head held high, Nikki breezed over
to the other side of Leon's to join Lacey
Dupree and Robin Fisher. She didn't
so much as glance at Brittany or Tim
again.

Tim's jaw tightened as he strode out of
the restaurant. The door slammed shut
behind him.

Brittany immediately turned to Kim.
"Why did you do *that*?" she cried.

"Do what?" Kim asked innocently.

"You know perfectly well what!" Brittany said, crossing her arms and slumping in

her seat. "Tim had no choice but to say he'd meet me at the dance tonight."

Kim seemed to be enjoying herself. "Is that so bad?"

"Yes!" Brittany said through clenched teeth.

Kim finished her drink. "You've been dying to go out with Tim again. Now you've got another chance."

"I wanted it to be *his* idea!" Brittany pointed out. "Not yours."

"What does it matter whose idea it is?" Kim asked with a shrug. "Now everything's up to you."

Brittany sighed. Kim was right, she supposed. Now she sort of had a date to the dance, and she *would* be with Tim Cooper. She looked over her shoulder at Nikki. All in all, things could be worse.

Kim leaned closer. "Did you see the look on Nikki's face when she spotted you and Tim together?"

"She did nearly die, didn't she," Brittany said slowly. She started thinking about the night ahead. This was her big chance, all right. And she wasn't going to blow it. Not this time.

"Let's go," she said to Kim, leaving some money on the table and grabbing her bag. There wasn't much time left before the dance, and she had some serious shopping to do. Then there were her hair and makeup. She'd have to be an absolute knockout. Tim Cooper, Brittany knew, wasn't the kind of guy who'd fall for her easily.

8 〜〜〜

"You're not going to the dance? Why not?" Kim's voice crackled sharply over the telephone wires.

Samantha flopped back on her bed. "I guess I'm just not in a dancing mood," she said vaguely as she pulled on the phone cord and walked over to the mirror. She looked like a washout. Sighing, she picked up a cosmetics brush and started working blusher onto her cheeks.

Kim wasn't about to be put off, as usual. "So what *are* you going to do tonight—sit at home and study French again?"

"Of course not! It's Friday night," Samantha replied. She wasn't going to tell Kim about her new plan. Not yet.

"Well, I've worked everything out. Brittany and Tim are double-dating with Jeremy and me, so you could join us," Kim began.

"Thanks, Kim. That's very generous of you, but I think I'll pass," Samantha said firmly, adding a little mascara.

"I'm only trying to help." Kim sounded angry.

"I know that. I appreciate all the trouble you're going through for me, really," Samantha lied. "But I honestly do have plans of my own tonight."

"With Marc LeBlanc?" Kim asked with more than a trace of sarcasm.

"That remains to be seen," Samantha replied mysteriously.

"Oh, Samantha, come on," Kim said. "I've told you already. *Forget him.*"

"Look, Kim, I've really got to run," Samantha said coolly. A huge gob of mascara had landed on her nose. Samantha reached for her makeup remover. "I'll talk to you later, okay?"

"It's your funeral," Kim muttered as Samantha hung up.

She pushed Kim's warning out of her mind and got down on the floor to wiggle into her tight black jeans. They made her look so much thinner, she told herself.

Then she hobbled to her dresser and pulled out her favorite fluorescent pink sweater. A few minutes later, she was ready to go.

Outside, the night was calm and still as Samantha pulled on her leather gloves and finished buttoning her long black coat. It was cold, but what a perfect night for a romantic evening with Marc! Humming to herself, she climbed behind the wheel of her mother's car. Fortunately, the heater was working.

Samantha's first stop was the ice-cream parlor where she had first met Marc the past weekend. Maybe he'd show up there again. Pulling into the small lot, she glanced at the parked vehicles but didn't see his little car.

"Give him time," she told herself, getting out of her car. "It's still early."

Samantha hurried toward the door of the ice-cream parlor. She couldn't really imagine eating ice cream on a cold night like that, but she was ready to brave anything for Marc.

Inside the little shop, she ordered a French vanilla cone. Then she sat down at a table near the window, slowly licking her ice cream and watching the parking lot. Marc didn't show up. In fact, no one did. She felt a little self-conscious sitting all alone, but she gritted her teeth and kept one eye on the door.

Eventually a few parents wandered in with their children, but after nearly an hour of waiting, Samantha's ice-cream cone was long gone and so was her patience. Obviously Marc wasn't going to show up. Coming to the ice-cream parlor had been a crazy idea, anyway.

Sighing, Samantha stuffed her hands in her pockets and walked outside. Just two doors down was a small theater that showed foreign films. According to the marquee, that night's movie was French.

Of course! If Marc was anywhere, he'd be in that theater! Without a moment's hesitation, Samantha ran toward the box office, envisioning herself bumping into Marc. He'd be alone, naturally, and he'd offer her a seat. Then she'd lean close enough to smell his cologne, his strong arm encircling her shoulders. . . .

"How many?"

"Wh-what?" Samantha stammered, her daydream fading as she realized that the girl selling tickets was staring at her.

"Tickets? How many do you want?"

"Oh, just one," Samantha said quickly, sliding a bill under the window.

"You'd better hurry. The show's about

to start," the girl said as she slipped a ticket and some change to Samantha.

Samantha shoved open the door and was greeted by the smell of popcorn and hot dogs. She made her way into the darkened auditorium just as the credits began to roll.

Now, where to sit? Standing at the top of the aisle as her eyes adjusted to the darkness, Samantha tried to find Marc in the audience. It was nearly impossible to see. Slowly she started down the aisle, hoping to catch a glimpse of his profile.

"Samantha, is that you?"

Her heart nearly stopped. Marc? She turned and saw someone waving to her from the third row. Sudden bright light from the screen illuminated his face, and Samantha's hopes plummeted. Kyle Kirkwood. The guy was turning up everywhere she went. Samantha shuddered as she remembered that horrible, mercifully short ride in his truck.

Kyle was seated on the aisle, munching from a huge tub of oily popcorn.

"Hi," Samantha said weakly.

"Are you here alone?" he asked.

Samantha cringed. What if someone from school saw her talking to a nerd?

"I—I'm meeting someone," she stammered.

Kyle looked a little disappointed. "Oh. I, uh, thought you could sit here. If you wanted to, I mean." In the semidarkness his eyebrows rose slightly. "Your friend, too."

What could she say? Kyle *had* been kind enough to give her a ride home, and she hadn't been very nice to him. Still—he was a definite social zero, and her reputation could be at stake. "Maybe I will," she lied, "but first I'd better try to find my friend." She offered Kyle a frozen smile as someone shushed her from the second row. She felt a little twinge of guilt as she turned away. Kyle was a nice enough guy. It was too bad he was such a brain.

Samantha walked down the rest of the aisle, then up the other side of the auditorium, but there was no sign of Marc. The theater was as big a flop as the ice-cream parlor. Why had she ever thought she could find him on a Friday night in River Heights, anyway? Maybe she should have tried the Westmoor campus, or . . .

Someone told her to sit down. Samantha was trapped.

With a sinking sensation in her stomach, she took a seat near the back. At least she could watch anyone coming into the theater. The movie seemed like a real bore, and the subtitles were distracting. Folding her arms across her chest, Samantha tried to follow the action on the screen.

Sure enough, the movie was totally dull. Even the lead, a famous French star, wasn't that exciting looking. In Samantha's opinion, he didn't hold a candle to Marc LeBlanc.

Samantha settled back in her seat. The theater was dark and warm, and she yawned lazily. Briefly she considered going to the refreshment stand and getting a diet soda, but she decided it was too much trouble. Instead, she closed her eyes for a moment and imagined that she and Marc, not the actress and actor on the screen, were involved in an exciting romantic adventure.

Smiling to herself, she kept her eyes closed and let the fantasy play through her mind. She and Marc were stranded alone on a remote tropical island. . . .

"Samantha?"

"Mmm?" she murmured. Why was Marc shaking her like that?

"Samantha, wake up!"

"What?" Samantha's eyes flew open and she realized with a shock that Kyle Kirkwood was standing directly over her.

His hand was on her shoulder, and his face was pressed close to hers.

Samantha tried not to panic. The house-lights were on, and the auditorium was practically empty.

"Are you okay?" Kyle asked, sounding concerned.

"Oh, yes. I mean, I guess I just dropped off for a while."

Kyle smiled, and Samantha had to admit that he was almost cute—in a nerdy sort of way, of course.

"You did more than drop off," Kyle told her. "You were snoring!"

"I was *not*—" Samantha started to protest, but she saw that his eyes were glinting mischievously.

Kyle nodded toward the exit. "Come on, I'll buy you a cup of coffee to wake you up."

No way was she going anywhere with Kyle the Brain! One ride in his awful truck had been plenty, thank you very much. And yet—Kyle was offering her that sweet off-center smile—there was something a tiny bit appealing about the guy. He probably wasn't so bad, even if he was a nerd with a capital *N*.

"I really have to get going," Samantha said apologetically.

"Sure," he said, smiling slightly. "I understand."

As they walked to the lobby, Samantha felt another pang of guilt. She really hadn't meant to hurt Kyle's feelings. Who would ever find out she'd had a cup of coffee with him, for heaven's sake?

They stepped outside, and cold air surrounded Samantha. She rubbed her arms. "Look, maybe coffee would be okay—"

"Don't do me any favors," he replied lightly.

Samantha smiled her most winning smile. "Oh, no, Kyle—I mean it. I'd love some coffee."

He frowned as if he was trying to decide if she was sincere. "How about the doughnut shop across the street?" he suggested finally.

"That sounds wonderful," Samantha said quickly. She knew no one ever hung out at that doughnut shop.

As they headed across the street to the small building with a flickering green-and-pink neon sign, Samantha noticed the sign: "Jasper's Doughnuts—the Best in the World."

"I want you to know, that's not false advertising," Kyle said. He opened the door for Samantha, and a small brass bell mounted on the frame rang softly. At least the nerd had manners, Samantha told herself.

Inside the old-fashioned café, the scent of coffee, cinnamon, and chocolate mingled in the air. According to the menu posted over the counter, Jasper's served pastry, espresso, and coffees from around the world.

Samantha slid into a well-worn booth, and Kyle sat on the bench across from her. His hair seemed blonder right then for some reason. The light dusting of freckles across the bridge of his nose made him look almost cute—in a geeky way, of course.

Kyle glanced up from the menu. "You might try the Brazilian coffee and a chocolate éclair—or maybe a lemon-filled cream puff."

Samantha rubbed her cold hands. Obviously she couldn't worry about her figure right then. She'd already blown it with the ice cream earlier. "Anything," she said out loud, "as long as it's hot."

"And guaranteed to wake you up," Kyle said, motioning to the waitress.

"You've been here a lot?" Samantha asked after the woman left with their orders.

Kyle nodded. "About once a week, actually. Whenever there's a new foreign film at the theater."

"And I figured that you were always studying," Samantha said before she could stop herself.

Kyle chuckled. "Everyone needs a break," he said as the waitress brought their coffee.

Samantha laced her fingers around the warm cup and let the aromatic steam waft up to her nose. She took a sip of coffee and watched Kyle over the rim of her cup. He was obviously nervous. She could tell by the way he held his coffee cup—in a death grip that turned his knuckles white. She didn't blame him, really. They both knew they were miles apart socially.

But, Samantha realized, sipping the strong Brazilian blend, she wasn't having such an awful time. She decided to enjoy the rest of the evening, Marc LeBlanc or no Marc LeBlanc.

Over the thrum of the music and the flash of the revolving lights, Brittany noticed that Jeremy seemed restless. He scowled as he scanned the crowd of dancing kids on the gym floor. "I told you," he said to Kim. "Nerd-o-rama."

Kim laughed, but Brittany didn't join in.

Where was Tim? He was supposed to have met her an hour ago. Maybe he wasn't going to show up. What would Jeremy and Kim think if she, Brittany Tate, were stood up? But that was impossible. She glanced nervously at the door.

"So where's Cooper?" Jeremy asked, as if he had read Brittany's thoughts.

"Oh, he'll be here," Kim said. "He's the kind of guy who keeps his word."

Brittany nodded silently. The music throbbed around them, and the dance floor was packed. A number of kids were leaning against the walls or hanging around the refreshment table. Brittany would rather die than stand on the sidelines and watch the action. She put what she hoped was a bored expression on her face and steeled herself against glancing at her watch. He'll show up, she told herself. "He's been delayed, that's all."

The minutes passed. Finally Brittany decided she wasn't going to mope around and wait for Tim forever. "You two go ahead and dance," she said, flashing a smile at Kim and Jeremy. "I'll be fine. Really."

"Okay," Jeremy said, dragging Kim onto the dance floor. "See ya, Brittany," he called over his shoulder.

Brittany glanced around, trying not to look desperate. Ben Newhouse was standing near the band. He looked as if he needed some cheering up. Besides, she certainly didn't want Tim to come into the gym and discover her waiting for him.

Brittany breezed through the crowd, enjoying the admiring glances cast in her direction. And why not? Her hair, tousled in waves over her shoulders, looked terrific, and her outfit—a new one—had cost her a small fortune.

The red minidress shimmered under the lights, and the metallic thread that ran through the fabric matched her gold necklace and bracelets.

"Hi," she said, coming up to Ben.

He glanced her way but barely smiled. "Oh, hi, Brittany," he replied.

"Great dance," she said.

"If you say so." Ben's face was expressionless.

He was probably still depressed over Emily, Brittany figured. She tried again. "The band's not bad."

"I guess not."

Brittany seethed. Cheering up Ben was a lot harder than she had thought it would be. Why did she even bother?

"Do you want to dance?" Ben asked suddenly.

Brittany raised her eyebrows. "Sure, I'd love to."

It would serve Tim Cooper right. Brittany took Ben's hand and led him to a spot on the floor where Tim would be sure to see them the minute he walked in.

The music shifted suddenly, and the band began playing a slow tune. Couples drifted closer together. Ben put his arms around Brittany, but he didn't hold her very tightly. In fact, he barely touched her.

Brittany looked up at Ben questioningly. "I guess I'm not such great company," he said with a sigh.

You can say that again, Brittany thought.

"Emily and I broke up." The guy looked devastated.

"Oh, really? I didn't know," Brittany lied. "What happened?"

He glanced over her shoulder. "I'd rather not talk about it."

Brittany gritted her teeth. By the time the band had finished the song, she was totally bored. Obviously, Ben hadn't even noticed her new dress. He was saying something about Emily. Brittany barely heard him.

"I just can't get used to her moving to New York and dating other guys," Ben finally blurted out.

Now, *this* was more like it. "You mean

Jason Monroe?" Brittany prompted. If Emily had dated the star of "Three Strikes," Brittany wanted details.

Ben shook his head as the music picked up again. "Not him. Some friend of her mother's, though."

"Oh." Who cares? Brittany thought, glancing toward the door. Tim Cooper was just walking in. "Ben, I've got to go," she said quickly. "Thanks for the dance." She squeezed his hand before leaving him in the middle of the floor and wending her way through the crowd to Tim.

She couldn't help the telltale drumming of her heart. Tim looked fantastic in his blue corduroys and bright red sweater.

"Hi." Brittany greeted him, tossing her hair over her shoulder.

Tim gazed at her, but Brittany couldn't read his expression.

"Sorry I'm late," he said. "I had to wait for my mom to get home so I could borrow her car—"

"No problem," Brittany said breezily. "You're here now."

"Yep." Hands in his pockets, Tim stared past her to scan the crowd. With a sinking heart, Brittany realized that he was looking for Nikki.

What was the matter with these guys, anyway?

First Ben could do nothing but mope about Emily. Now, it seemed, Tim was still pining over Nikki. It was enough to make her sick.

Brittany slipped her arm through Tim's as the band launched into a Dead Beats tune. "Come on, let's dance."

"Sure." Tim nodded and allowed himself to be led onto the dance floor. Brittany whirled and twisted, putting in a lot of extra effort to get Tim's attention. He just seemed to be going through the motions, though.

Brittany knew that half the boys in the gym were watching her, but Tim didn't seem to notice. She spun around a few times, moving to the beat, but Tim's gaze kept wandering to the door.

Not again! Brittany was more than a little irritated. This was going to be a long night unless she could get Tim's mind off Nikki. And right then there didn't seem to be much chance of *that*.

9 ~~~~~~

Karen Jacobs felt totally out of place. She'd been to school dances before, of course, but she never got used to standing alone in a crowd near the door. As she listened to the pounding beat of the band and watched the couples dance, she got more and more depressed. And, to make matters worse, Ben Newhouse had danced with Brittany Tate!

Fortunately, though, Karen told herself, Ben didn't seem to be having that good a time. He never so much as smiled.

Karen wandered closer to the band as another song ended. Maybe she should just go home and end this torture. Seeing Brittany and Ben together was almost worse than watching him with Emily had been.

Karen sighed as she glanced down at her mint green dress. She'd been a fool to think that with a little makeup and a new outfit, she'd be able to impress Ben.

"Karen?"

She recognized Ben's voice instantly. Whirling around, Karen found him standing right behind her.

"Hi," she said, flustered. Automatically she looked past Ben for Brittany, but Ben was alone. Brittany, thank heaven, was on the far side of the gym, turning her megawatt charm on Tim Cooper. The girl never quit.

"I didn't think you'd be here," Ben said as another song started up.

"It was kind of a last-minute decision," Karen said shyly.

Ben shrugged. "Well, do you want to dance?"

Karen nodded. "Sure," she said, catching her breath as Ben took her hand and led her onto the floor. Was this really happening? Her heart soared with new hope, and her fingers tingled where they touched his.

They danced almost every dance for the next hour or so. Karen was ecstatic. Maybe her luck was finally turning.

Just as Karen thought that things couldn't be more perfect, Ben asked over the music, "Would you like to grab a hamburger at the Loft?"

Karen's spirits skyrocketed right through the roof of the gym. "That'd be great," she said.

Ben smiled, his usual heartwarming smile. "Okay, let's go."

"Just give me a minute to get my coat," Karen said quickly. She hurried to the rest room, then found a pay phone to call her mother and explain that she had a ride home. She hurried back to the gym, where Ben was waiting—for her.

For a few seconds Karen was afraid Ben might have changed his mind. But, no, there he was, leaning against the wall talking to Rick Stratton and Lacey Dupree. Karen breathed a sigh of relief.

In the car Karen was careful not to sit too close to Ben. She didn't want to scare him off. What if he realized she had a major crush on him? Didn't guys hate that sort of thing?

Ben drove through the quiet streets, and the interior of the little car felt warm and cozy. Karen settled back in the seat happily.

As Ben pulled into the parking lot of the Loft, he sighed. "Emily and I used to come here all the time," he said softly.

Karen's bubble of joy burst. She glanced at Ben. Even in the darkness she could see the traces of sadness near his mouth and eyes. "Maybe we should go somewhere else," she suggested.

Ben shook his head and reached for the door. "Nope. I may as well face facts. Emily and I are through for good."

"I'm a good listener," Karen said quickly. "I mean, if you want to talk about it."

Ben cleared his throat. "You might be bored."

"Oh, no," Karen lied. "Please let me help."

A blast of cold air swirled into the warm car as Ben opened the door. Karen's spirits sank. Ben wasn't interested in her. He only wanted to talk to someone about Emily.

They walked across the parking lot and up the stairs to the entrance. Lots of kids were already inside.

Karen told herself to be patient. Ben would need time to get over Emily. But, she vowed, he would *never* find out that she was in love with him. *Never.*

Brittany did her best to draw Tim into a real conversation. She smiled, she flirted, she put her head on his shoulder when they danced, but she knew he just wasn't interested.

Of course Nikki Masters had shown up at the dance. Brittany cringed each time Tim's gaze wandered toward Nikki as boy after boy asked her to dance. She's not worth it, Brittany wanted to scream. The girl is a total fraud. What was wrong with Tim—was he *blind?*

Kim and Jeremy, arms linked, threaded their way through the crowd toward Brittany and Tim. "We're going over to Commotion," Kim called. "Want to join us?"

Brittany brightened. At last she had a chance to get Tim far away from Nikki. "Sure," she replied brightly. Then she glanced at Tim. "I mean, if *you* want to, of course."

Tim's gaze fairly burned across the dance floor, past several couples to Nikki. She was dancing wildly in a simple black dress, as if she didn't have a care in the world. Mark Giordano, the center of the football team, was her current partner. Her blond hair gleamed nearly silver under the lights.

"Tim?" Brittany asked again, her lower lip protruding a bit.

He turned back to her as if he'd forgotten she existed. "What?"

Brittany seethed, but she kept her voice light. "Jeremy and Kim are going to Commotion. They asked us to go with them."

"Oh, right." Tim flashed Brittany a smile and some of her anger disappeared. "Why not?" He glanced back one more time at Nikki, then took Brittany's elbow and propelled her out of the gym—right past Lara Bennett.

Lara's mouth rounded as she saw Tim and Brittany together. "Are you leaving already?" she asked, obviously disappointed.

Brittany tossed her a pitying smile. "It's time to move on," she said, hoping Lara would catch her real meaning. One never knew with sophomores.

Lara blushed. "Oh. Right."

Tim smiled at the little dip as Brittany grabbed her coat. "See you later," he said. Lara visibly brightened. Brittany was actually embarrassed for her.

Outside, Tim took Brittany's arm, and she sighed in relief. Oh, please, Brittany thought. Forget Nikki Masters!

Tim settled Brittany into his mom's Ford Taurus as Jeremy's Porsche flew by. It skidded a little as it rounded a corner much too fast. Tim visibly blanched as the Porsche squealed.

"He should be more careful. It's cold and there's a thin layer of ice on the roads," Tim said, frowning.

"It's just his style," Brittany said, waving her hand airily.

"He could end up getting hurt," Tim pointed out.

"I don't think Jeremy Pratt thinks much about getting hurt," Brittany said lightly, trying to shake Tim out of his serious mood.

Tim said nothing as he started the car and slowly pulled out of the parking lot.

Jeremy and Kim would be at Commotion ages before she and Tim got there, but Brittany didn't mind. At least she'd have more time alone with him, and that was exactly what she wanted. Unfortunately, Tim wasn't saying much, so Brittany kept chattering away about nothing in particular.

Inside, Commotion was hopping. A live band was blaring from the stage, and kids were dancing on the main dance floor as well as the platforms near the stage. Huge black-and-white posters of frantic crowds hung on the walls.

The lights were constantly flashing, and Brittany had to squint through the crowd.

"Hey, Brittany, Tim! Over here!" Kim waved from a small table near the refreshment counters. She and Jeremy were seated close together, and Jeremy had his arm slung over the back of her chair.

"What took you so long?" Jeremy asked as Brittany and Tim came up.

Tim shrugged. "I value my life."

Jeremy's blond brows shot up. "What do you mean, Cooper?"

"I drive carefully," Tim said flatly.

What a dumb thing to say! Brittany didn't want to see Jeremy and Tim start throwing verbal punches at each other. "Let's get something to eat," she suggested, eager to change the subject. "I'm starving."

"Me, too," Kim agreed quickly. "How about some nachos and sodas?"

Without a word, both Tim and Jeremy headed over to the snack bar.

Kim and Brittany immediately made their way in the opposite direction to the ladies' room. Surprisingly they seemed to have the place to themselves. Brittany went straight for the mirror and studied her reflection with a critical eye.

"So how's it going?" Kim asked, reaching into her tiny bag for her comb.

"Not great," Brittany admitted. Sighing, she brushed her hair until it shone. "Tim's still hung-up on Nikki."

"That's no problem," Kim said with a

shrug. She touched up her mascara, then added a little lavender shadow to her eyelids. "Turn up the old Tate heat."

"I've tried," Brittany said. "Believe me."

"Just give it time," Kim said airily. "By the end of the night," Kim went on, adjusting her crimson sweater, "Tim won't even remember Nikki's name."

That was encouraging. Brittany checked her lipstick and hoped that Tim Cooper was worth the extra effort. She was beginning to doubt it.

As the ladies' room door closed behind Brittany and Kim, Robin Fisher breathed out loud. Neither Kim nor Brittany had guessed that she was in one of the stalls and had heard their entire conversation.

The next morning the phone near Nikki's bed jangled insistently.

"Go away," Nikki said, squirming farther down under her covers. She finally answered on the fourth ring. "Hello?"

"Oh, Nikki!" Robin said breathlessly. "I just had to talk to you right away."

Nikki sat up quickly. "Why? What happened?"

"It's about Tim and Brittany."

"Don't remind me," Nikki said with a groan. "I saw them at the dance."

"It's not what you think," Robin assured her. She repeated what she'd overheard in the ladies' room at Commotion. "I'm telling you, Nikki, I watched them together for the rest of the night. Tim hardly said a word to Brittany. You have nothing to worry about, really."

Nikki sighed and stared out her bedroom window. "It doesn't matter."

"Of course it does," Robin insisted.

"No," Nikki said. "What Tim does with his life is his business." Her gaze focused on the gazebo where she'd had her talk with Tim only a few days before.

"Well, if you say so," Robin said slowly. "I'm just reporting what I saw."

"Thanks," Nikki said with a sigh.

"Listen, Nikki, how about meeting me at the mall this afternoon?" Robin asked. "Lacey gets off work at Platters at three."

"I'd like to, really," Nikki said honestly, "but my grandfather's stopping by this afternoon."

"You'll be missing out on a great sale at Glad Rags," Robin told her.

Nikki laughed. "Maybe next time, Rob."

"Okay. I'll see you Monday, then. Let me know if anything exciting happens, okay?"

Nikki said goodbye and hung up.

What she had told Robin was absolutely true. Tim Cooper didn't matter to her anymore. In fact, Brittany Tate was welcome to him. It was time, Nikki reminded herself, to get on with her life.

10

Her plan was working perfectly, Samantha thought during French class the next Tuesday. For the past two days, her daily quiz grades had dropped dramatically. Monsieur LeBlanc was beginning to notice her at last.

At the end of class he called Samantha up to his desk. "What's going on, Samantha?" he asked after the last student had filed out the door. His gaze was steady.

Samantha smiled sweetly. "Why, nothing, Monsieur LeBlanc."

"Nothing?" He raised a skeptical brow. "Last week you were near the top of the class. The lowest grade you received was"—he checked his grade book—"an A-minus. But *this* week . . ." A little crease developed between the teacher's eyebrows. "Your grades have plunged. Today you got an F."

Samantha tried to look devastated.

"What's happening?" Marc asked again, his voice soft and gentle. Samantha practically swooned.

"I—I don't know," she lied, hoping she sounded confused.

"Is there trouble at home?" Marc pressed.

"Oh, no!" Samantha answered.

The teacher looked thoughtful. "Maybe a problem with a boyfriend, then?"

"Oh, no. I'm not even going out with anybody right now," Samantha replied. Then she wondered whether she might have made herself sound a little *too* available.

Marc's eyes narrowed slightly. "Well, a student doesn't nosedive from an A to an F without a reason."

Samantha pouted a little, the way Brittany did when she wanted something. "Well, I had a lot of homework yesterday and over the weekend—from my other classes, I mean. French just seems to have gotten so much harder this week." She dimpled prettily as her accent moved farther and farther south.

Marc slowly pushed himself out of his chair. Standing directly across from him, Samantha felt her breath constrict in her lungs.

"Is it me?" Marc asked finally.

He'd guessed! Samantha felt a blush climb steadily up her neck. "Well, um——"

Sighing, Marc raked a hand through his hair. "Maybe I'm not explaining things clearly enough——"

"Oh, no!" she assured him hastily. Couldn't he feel the chemistry between them? Her heart was beating rapidly, and her hands were positively wet. "You're a *wonderful* teacher."

Marc frowned. "But the last couple of days you've been having trouble following along in class. Perhaps I'm going too quickly."

"No, no," Samantha said. "It's me. Maybe——maybe I need some special help."

"Special help?" the teacher said slowly.

"Tutoring maybe," Samantha suggested.

Marc glanced at her. "You know, Samantha, maybe that's not such a bad idea."

Here was her chance. Samantha swallowed hard and tried to look extremely vulnerable. "I'm really worried about my grades, Monsieur LeBlanc," she practically whispered. "My mom and dad will just die if I flunk."

"Then we won't let you," Marc said, offering her a sudden, dazzling smile. "There's nothing I can do today, of course, so you'll just have to study extra hard tonight. I'll talk to you about this again in a day or two." He reached for his jacket and rounded the desk.

"Thank you so much," Samantha said happily. Marc was *going to tutor her!* She'd finally be alone with him. She couldn't wait. He'd touch her hand, whisper her name, and then they would kiss. . . .

"You're welcome, Samantha." The teacher touched her lightly on the shoulder, and she tingled where his fingers had rested for the briefest second. "You've got a good ear for French. I want to get you through this."

Samantha beamed up at Marc LeBlanc and nearly floated out of the door.

Brittany was waiting for her in the hall. "What was *that* all about?" she asked, not the least bit concerned when the second bell rang.

Samantha raised her brows. "Well, Brittany, it seems that Monsieur LeBlanc has taken a sudden interest in me. In fact, we're going to be spending a lot of time alone together in the near future."

Brittany's mouth dropped open. "You're kidding! How'd you pull that off?"

Samantha smiled mysteriously. "Come on, Brittany, we're going to be late." She began to hurry down the hall, with Brittany at her heels. Samantha couldn't have been more satisfied. Things were finally beginning to work out the way *she* wanted them to.

Ben walked slowly down the hall. For practically the first time in his life, he felt lonely. He'd always been popular, a guy people looked up to. He was a good student and a pretty fair athlete. He was junior-class president and was in charge of loads of extracurricular activities. Now he was miserable.

Emily had been gone about five days, and he couldn't quit thinking or talking about her. He felt turned inside out.

Now he could tell that he was beginning to annoy some of his friends by constantly talking about her.

The only person who seemed willing to listen was Karen Jacobs, a girl he'd always thought of as a friend. Karen was smart enough and cute in her own way, but she didn't have Emily's spark. Emily was so lively and cheerful and—

Stop it, Newhouse, he told himself, heading toward the *Record* office.

Inside the newsroom, students were busy at typewriters or laying out photos.

Ben looked around until he spotted Karen, her head bent over a sports page. She was at a table near the back of the room.

Ben watched her work for a few minutes. Karen was Emily's opposite in a lot of ways. She obviously didn't spend much time on makeup or hair or clothes, but she was hardworking, sweet, and dependable.

He walked up behind her. "Karen?"

She nearly jumped off her little stool. Her head whipped around, and the faintest tinge colored her cheeks. "Oh, Ben, hi," she said, obviously flustered. She picked up a rag and started wiping her fingers. "What's up?"

Ben hesitated. He shouldn't have walked in and disturbed Karen like this.

"I thought I'd get an update on the Winter Carnival stuff we discussed," he said.

"Oh."

Did she sound just a little disappointed?

"Well, let's see," Karen said, squaring her shoulders. "We have an ad that'll go in the *Record* this week. I've asked the art department to come up with something a little flashier for the next edition." She picked up her knapsack from the floor and began riffling through one of her many notebooks. "Here. I have a copy of it."

Ben read the advertisement and nodded. "This is great."

"Then I've got some freshmen and sophomores working on posters that we'll put up in the mall and downtown," Karen went on. "Then, I think, we can start asking for donations."

Ben was impressed. "You're really into this," he said.

"Just doing my job." Karen started to smile, but it quickly fell away as she looked past Ben's shoulder.

"Hi," Brittany Tate chirped as Ben turned around. "What's going on?"

"I was just checking on some of the committee work for the carnival. It looks as if Karen's got donations and publicity under control. By the way, how are decorations coming?"

Brittany didn't miss a beat. She waved nonchalantly. "Oh, they'll be fine. But it'll be a lot of work—without Emily," she added nastily.

Ben felt a familiar jab of pain, but he

shrugged. "I'm sorry. I was hoping that you could get some of your friends to help. You have a lot of influence, you know," Ben pointed out. A little flattery went a long way with Brittany. "I'm sure people will help you."

Brittany shrugged. "I guess you're right."

Ben turned back to Karen. He had the feeling she'd been staring at him, though she quickly averted her eyes. "Karen, thanks for all your help," he said.

"Oh, Ben," Brittany said, as if she'd suddenly thought of something. "I found a picture you must have lost."

"A picture?" he repeated, puzzled.

Brittany pulled something out of her purse. A snapshot of Emily, Ben realized. The pain ripped through him again.

"I found this on my desk," Brittany said casually. "You know, when I was going to do that personality profile on Emily. I thought it might be yours."

Behind Ben, Karen Jacobs looked as if she might choke. Ben took the picture and turned it over. He recognized the photo, of course. He and Emily had been decorating the gym for last year's Valentine's Day dance. But someone had cut him from the picture. He frowned. Who would do something like that?

Probably Emily, he told himself. For her wallet or something.

"You found that on your desk?" Karen asked. Her face was suddenly pale.

Brittany tossed her hair back from her face. "Mmm. Funny, isn't it?"

"Not very," Karen said almost in a whisper. She seemed about to say more, but just then DeeDee Smith came over to the three of them.

"Hey, Brittany," DeeDee said, "I think I have a new idea for those personality pieces of yours."

Brittany's brows lifted politely, but she didn't seem very happy.

"You know, it might even make for an entire article," DeeDee said, thinking aloud. "Why don't we discuss it now? I've got a few minutes."

"Oh, sure," Brittany said, looking straight at Karen.

DeeDee looked pleased. "Great. Come on over to my area." She took Brittany by the elbow and steered her toward the far side of the room.

Ben turned back to Karen. "Okay. Well, I guess I'll see you later, right?"

Karen bit her lower lip. "Right." She turned back to her work as Ben left the newsroom. How could she have thought, even for a minute, that Ben had come to the *Record* office to see her? If DeeDee hadn't shown up, Brittany might have ruined her chances with Ben forever.

Karen gritted her teeth. Someday Brittany Tate would be very, very sorry.

The next day Samantha's hands practically shook as she slid her French test onto Monsieur LeBlanc's desk, facedown. The test had been harder than she'd expected. She'd finished the multiple-choice questions haphazardly and attempted a few verb conjugations, but she hadn't even tried to answer the short essays.

She was certain she'd failed. That was good *and* bad. Her plan to get the teacher's attention was working, all right, but she didn't want to flunk the class. What if Marc figured out what she was doing?

The teacher didn't waste any time. He picked up Samantha's test paper the minute she returned to her seat. She watched as he corrected her paper. The other students, even Kyle and Nikki, were still finishing up.

He frowned, and Samantha's stomach tightened. This *had* to work! Too much was at stake for her plan to fail now.

Finally he finished grading her paper and picked up another. When the bell rang and everyone was heading out the door, he beckoned Samantha up to his desk.

She crossed her fingers.

"Frankly, Samantha," the teacher said as she approached, "I'm shocked." He paused. "You really blew this test." He handed the pages back to her, and she cringed inwardly. Thirty-five points out of a possible one hundred! Maybe she'd overdone it.

"You didn't even try the essay questions," Monsieur LeBlanc pointed out.

"They were too difficult," Samantha told him, making her eyes as wide as possible.

"But some of these questions were a review of the material we studied last week—when your grades were in the stratosphere," Monsieur LeBlanc said, sounding puzzled.

He *had* noticed the good grades! But only after she'd let her class standing hit rock bottom. "I know," she said meekly. "I guess I forgot."

"There's another test coming up soon."

Samantha nodded.

"It'll be worth one-third of your grade. You'll have to work extremely hard to pass."

"Oh, I will," she promised.

The teacher leaned back in his chair. "Then we'd better see that you receive tutoring."

"I'm sure that would help a lot," Samantha assured him.

Monsieur LeBlanc eyed his desk calendar. "When do you have free time?"

"Any night," Samantha said quickly.

The teacher raised his eyebrows. "After school?"

"Yes," Samantha replied. "I mean, no. After dinner would be better."

"I'll work something out," Monsieur LeBlanc said, jotting a note to himself. He tucked the note into his grade book and reached for his jacket.

"Thank you so much," Samantha said as they headed for the door together.

"No problem." Marc smiled at her then. It wasn't just his friendly-teacher smile, either, Samantha told herself. No, this time his eyes were definitely sparkling. Samantha was sure there was a deeper meaning in his expression. He really cared about her, she knew.

"Don't worry, Samantha," Marc said. "We'll get through this."

We certainly will, Samantha thought happily. Together.

11

The next morning Samantha nearly fainted in the hall beside her locker.

"Y-you're my tutor?" she stammered, staring in disbelief at Kyle Kirkwood. He was leaning against a bank of lockers, grinning at her. It had to be some kind of cruel joke!

"In the flesh," Kyle replied with a shrug.

"But I thought Monsieur LeBlanc would be tutoring me." Surely there was some mistake, Samantha told herself. Don't panic.

"Well, he phoned me last night and asked me to help out." Kyle shifted the heavy textbooks under his arm. "He said this was *your* idea, by the way."

"Well, it was," Samantha admitted, glancing helplessly around the now-empty hallway. The last bell had rung.

"And you do need help," Kyle went on.

"Yes, I do, but—"

Kyle's eyes narrowed. "Look, Samantha, I'd be happy to help you out. But if you don't think I can do the job for some reason, then just forget it, okay?"

"No! I mean, I'm sure you'd do a great job," Samantha said, confused. She glanced down the empty hallway again, making absolutely sure she and Kyle were alone. She didn't want anyone to see her with Kyle, of course, but she honestly didn't want to hurt his feelings, either.

"Okay," Kyle said. "Suppose I stop by your house around seven-thirty tonight, then? We can study there or go to the library or wherever you want. I'll see you later."

Samantha nodded distractedly as Kyle took off down the hall. This wasn't what was supposed to happen! How could she possibly make Marc LeBlanc fall in love with her when she was going to be spending all her free time with Kyle the Brain?

Totally depressed, Samantha started toward her homeroom. There had to be some way to ditch Kyle and get back on course with Marc. Maybe if Kyle wasn't getting through to her, if her grades didn't improve, then Marc would realize that he, and he alone, could guide her through the treacherous French jungle.

That night Kyle arrived on the Daleys' doorstep at seven-thirty sharp. Samantha hesitated when he suggested they study at the library.

If anyone spotted them together, Samantha knew her social reputation would never be the same. She eyed his sloppy red high-top sneakers and sighed. She was going to have to make the best of a bad situation.

Outside, the stars twinkled overhead and a pale moon cast cool shadows over the neighborhood. It was a perfectly romantic evening, Samantha thought, and totally wasted. She slid a nervous glance in Kyle's direction as he drove through the quiet streets. He was staring straight ahead and saying very little. Was he nervous? Samantha wondered. She certainly was.

At the library Kyle guided Samantha to a back room with only a couple of tables. Good, Samantha thought. There would be much less risk of their being seen. On the other hand, she added to herself, no one from school was likely to see them. No one who counted, anyway.

They spent almost two hours working. Kyle seemed surprised that Samantha knew more than her grades showed.

"So what happened to you during the test?" he asked, puzzled.

Samantha sighed. "I guess I just froze."

"But you really seem to know this stuff."

"I know." Samantha avoided Kyle's penetrating gaze. "I really can't explain it," she said, doodling on a piece of scratch paper.

To her astonishment, Kyle placed his hand over hers. "You know, I'll bet you can ace the next test. In fact, I *know* so. All you have to do is put in a little extra effort." He smiled, his dimple creasing. "Come on. Let's get out of here and get some coffee or something."

Samantha wanted to decline politely, but she just couldn't bring herself to say no. "At Jasper's?" she asked.

He grinned. "Where else?"

"So where were *you* all weekend?" Brittany demanded on Monday.

Samantha swallowed hard. She couldn't let Brittany know that she was spending her time with Kyle Kirkwood, for heaven's sake. Brittany would think she'd gone off the deep end. Besides, she didn't want anyone to guess that she was actually starting to look forward to the tutoring sessions and the coffee and doughnuts afterward.

But having coffee with Kyle didn't mean she was *dating* the guy, Samantha reminded herself for the millionth time. He hadn't tried to kiss her—not that he'd even think of it, of course. At school Kyle kept his distance, thank heaven.

"So?" Brittany prodded, startling Samantha from her thoughts.

"So—what?" Samantha said, shutting her locker carefully.

"Where have you been?" Brittany asked again, sounding impatient.

Samantha thought fast. "Oh, in the library. Studying. I'm having some trouble in French, and I'm working really hard." There was no reason to bring up Kyle.

Kim, who had been hurrying toward them, caught the tail end of their conversation. "Speaking of French," she said with a grin, "how's it going with Monsieur *LeLove*?"

Samantha bristled. "Just fine, thank you."

Kim drew one hand through her shiny blond hair. "Has he actually asked you out yet?"

"Well, um, no," Samantha admitted. "But—"

"Shh!" Brittany said suddenly. "He's coming this way."

To Samantha's horror, she spied Marc wending his way through a knot of students. He was heading straight toward her. He wouldn't bring up the fact that she was being tutored by Kyle, would he? She would just die. Desperately she glanced around for a means of escape.

"Samantha!" Marc called. "I've been looking everywhere for you!"

Kim's mouth dropped open in obvious disbelief. Brittany's eyes widened.

"You have?" Samantha asked, her heart hammering joyously. This was it. He'd finally realized he was in love with her!

"Yes. Actually, I was wondering if you'd be free Friday night." Marc seemed nervous.

"Well, yes, I think so—" Samantha said, flustered.

"Good," Marc replied, sounding relieved.

Samantha wanted to kiss him for showing his true feelings in front of her friends. She felt herself flush with pleasure.

Marc glanced from Kim to Brittany. Kim was staring at him as if he'd dropped in from some other planet.

"Uh, Samantha, can we talk alone?" he asked.

"Oh, sure—" Her spirits soaring, Samantha walked with Marc a little farther down the hall.

"Listen, I've got a problem," he said. "I promised I'd watch my sister's three-year-old daughter on Friday night. But now I've had a sudden change of plans and I can't. My sister is really in a bind, so I need someone to fill in and baby-sit for me. I really hate to ask you this, Samantha, but—"

"B-baby-sit?" Samantha said faintly.

"Well, yes. From about six-thirty until midnight or one." Marc flashed her his most charming smile. "You'd be a lifesaver if you could help out."

Brittany and Kim, who had strolled close enough to hear, exchanged glances. Brittany threw Samantha a pitying look, and Samantha wanted to drop through the floor. She'd never hear the end of this. Brittany and Kim would needle her forever.

Brittany stepped toward them quickly. "Excuse me, but you haven't forgotten, have you, Samantha? You can't possibly baby-sit Friday night!"

"I—I can't?" Samantha stammered.

"We're all going to Jeremy's party, remember?'' Brittany said. ''He'd be *so* hurt and disappointed if you didn't show up.''

Kim looked as if she were about to say something, but Brittany cast her a warning glance and she didn't even open her mouth.

Marc seemed disappointed. ''Oh, is that right?''

''It must have slipped my mind,'' Samantha replied, feeling a rush of gratitude toward Brittany. ''But I did say I'd go.''

Marc raked his fingers through his thick, unruly hair. ''I guess I'll just have to find someone else, then,'' he said.

Brittany smiled. ''Why not ask Nikki Masters?'' she offered, barely able to hide a smile. ''I hear she's great with kids.''

''Thanks, Brittany, I'll do that,'' Marc said, brightening. He waved and quickly took off down the hall. As soon as he had safely rounded the corner, Brittany started to howl with laughter. Kim joined in.

Samantha sagged against the wall. Her cheeks were burning, and tears of embarrassment filled the lower rims of her eyes. She blinked rapidly. ''Thanks, Brittany.''

''Anytime,'' Brittany gasped. ''I told you that guy wasn't for you. What a jerk.''

Kim actually seemed a little pleased by the way things had turned out. ''That's right. Teacher crushes are never a good idea."

Samantha's heart ached. Her friends were right, of course, but she knew it would take time before she was completely over Marc LeBlanc. She squared her shoulders. He had just made her look like a major fool, after all. And no guy messed with Samantha Daley.

"Samantha, are you okay?" Brittany asked, recovering from her outburst. "I'm sorry I laughed."

Samantha lifted her small chin. "It doesn't matter, really."

"Then you'll go to Jeremy's party?" Kim asked.

Samantha sighed heavily. "I guess so," she said. "But don't you *dare* set me up with Hal or Wayne." All three of them laughed this time, and Samantha began to feel a bit better.

Brittany glanced at her watch. "Look, I've got to run down to the *Record* office. I'll see you guys later, okay?" She gave a hurried wave and headed down the hall. As she pulled open the newsroom door, she came face-to-face with Karen Jacobs.

The other girl seemed to freeze. What was the matter with her anyway? Brittany wondered.

Brittany's reporter instinct clicked in,

and she smiled at Karen. "You look like you've just seen a ghost," she said.

Karen bit her lip. "Not exactly," she replied.

Brittany raised her eyebrows. It looked as if Karen Jacobs had just found out something extremely interesting.

"What's wrong?" Brittany pressed.

Karen stepped sideways. "I . . . I don't think I should tell you."

Brittany studied her, amazed. She could practically *smell* a story. "Why not?" she asked as Ben Newhouse joined them.

Ben must have seen the tortured look on Karen's face. "Hey, is anything wrong?" he asked.

"Everything," Karen replied, swallowing hard.

"What's that supposed to mean?" Ben said.

Karen looked at Brittany, but Brittany was determined to stick around. She wasn't about to miss *this,* whatever it was!

Karen took a deep breath. "I just heard something terrible!" she practically whispered.

"What?" Brittany demanded.

Karen ignored her and looked directly at Ben. "I'm not kidding." She rubbed her arms as if from a sudden chill. "Believe me, when this news gets out, River Heights High may never be the same!"

———————

Karen Jacobs has stumbled on a scandal that will rock the school. If she breaks the story, she's sure to be editor-in-chief the next year. But she'll also blow her chances with Ben Newhouse. What should she do? New British exchange student Niles Butler has caught Nikki Masters's eye. How can she have fallen in love again so quickly? Find out in River Heights #7, *Cheating Hearts*.